SNAPPED AND FRAMED!

A TAMSIN KERNICK ENGLISH COZY MYSTERY

BOOK 6

LUCY EMBLEM

ALSO BY LUCY EMBLEM

More mysteries with Quiz, Banjo, and Moonbeam

Where it all began ..

Sit, Stay, Murder!

Ready, Aim, Woof!

Down Dog!

Barks, Bikes, and Bodies!

Ma-ah, Ma-ah, Murder!

Snapped and Framed!

Christmas Carols and Canine Capers! A Howling Good Christmas Mystery!

CHAPTER ONE

"These photos are just so much better than mine," Tamsin said sadly, as she pushed her unruly dark hair behind her ear and flapped the latest copy of the *Malvern Mercury* in the air, managing to land it in her creamy walnut gateau and spattering icing about.

"Steady on!" said Emerald, as she reached her long slender arms forward to grab the flying newspaper, and tore off the loaded corner. "Jean-Philippe will throw us out of The Cake Stop if you carry on like that!"

Banjo and Quiz, Tamsin's collies, scrambled off their mats beside the café table and busily cleared up the crumbs that had fallen to the floor, tiny terrier Moonbeam ducking between their legs to snatch the morsels.

"It's an ill wind ..." Charity laughed as she watched, and urged Muffin off her lap to join in the foraging. Tamsin's three dogs left the floor spotless and returned to their dozing.

"Oh sorry! It's just so frustrating." Tamsin folded the remains of the paper carefully and deliberately, and showed her friends what she was looking at. "These are the photos Jeff took at my last *Top Dogs* walk - the one we did on Pinnacle Hill. They're just so good!"

"Well, they would be good, wouldn't they dear, seeing as he's the official photographer for the paper?" Charity, reasonable as ever, settled Muffin beside her again on the armchair. There was plenty of room for the fluffy little brown dog next to the old lady's diminutive body.

"You see, I need photos for my website and for flyers - to show people what fun my dog training really is, you know? And mine are just rubbish compared to Jeff's."

"This isn't like you, Tamsin! A challenge you're not rising to?" Emerald tossed her long blonde plait over her shoulder and gave a crooked smile.

"You're right, of course. I should see this as a sign from above."

"A sign that you need to get out there and learn how to do it yourself," said Charity encouragingly.

"There must be courses ... but I don't want to have to buy loads of super-expensive camera equipment. You've seen those big black bags Jeff humps round on his assignments?"

"I've got some good snaps on my smartphone recently," said Emerald thoughtfully. "I got Sara to take some of me practicing yoga last time she was home from college, so I could use the photos for publicity for my classes - like you. She's pretty good at it - got some nice pictures. Very clear."

"She probably has to learn how to take effective photos of trees and landscapes and whatnot, for her land management studies," said Charity.

"And conservation she does too. Probably very important to get that right," Tamsin took another mouthful of walnut cake, savoured it, then sat up straight with a sudden thought, "I wonder if Jean-Philippe knows anyone? The world and his wife visit The Cake Stop .."

"And don't forget the coffee shop underground network!" laughed Emerald. "Remember how helpful he was when he was able to tap into his network of café friends in that murder involving the environmentalists in Hereford?"

"The thought is father of the deed," Tamsin announced as she waved her hand towards the coffee shop counter, where Jean-Philippe was in casual conversation with his barista Kylie. He snapped to attention and shimmied across to their table.

"*Qu'est-ce que c'est?* There is something not right with the coffee?" he asked with great concern, his bushy black eyebrows knitting together.

"*Mais non!*" Tamsin was quick to reassure him. "Your offerings are always superb. Don't you notice how hard it is to keep us away?"

Jean-Philippe smiled. "I'd never want to keep you away. How boring my life would become without you plotting and scheming here at the window table. How can I help you?"

"You know everyone, Jean-Philippe. Though possibly not the same everyone that Charity knows," she nodded to her friend, who did indeed know everyone in the Malvern Hills - their faults, their foibles, their family histories. "And I wondered ... do you know of anyone who teaches photography? Not professional-type photography - rather, how to take successful pics on my phone?"

"*Mais oui!*" He thought for a moment, then said, "I think I can help you there! You remember my friend Jeremy, with the coffee shop in the Old Market centre in Hereford?"

Tamsin nodded enthusiastically, "Lovely fudge and chocolate cake!"

"You *would* remember that! *Eh bien,* he was telling me that he had a photography class running in his events room a few months ago. Brought a lot of customers to his café - they even had an exhibition. I must ask him who it was who ran the program. Perhaps they'd like to do one here?"

"Oh, they could use your upper room, Jean-Philippe, when I'm not using it for yoga classes!"

"What a great idea, Emerald," said Tamsin, looking like the cat that had got the cream. "Let us know what you find out, Jean-Philippe! It has to be simple photography, mind you. I can't be doing with f numbers and depth of field and exposures and all that. Just want some tricks to make my dog photos look better."

"You have no shortage of dogs to photograph," agreed Charity. "And you get plenty of happy, smiling owners too, having such fun with the way you teach."

"Thank you Charity! That means a lot to me. If I can help people treat their dogs with more respect and enjoy them as individuals - I've done my bit for dogdom." She leant back and folded her arms, then jumped forward again, "Oh! Oh my goodness! I haven't finished this delicious cake."

"I've never seen you distracted from cake before," laughed Jean-Philippe as he gave the table a quick wipe, swished his tea-towel over his shoulder, and turned back to help Kylie with the small queue that had gathered at the counter - of ruddy-faced hill-walkers with poles and rucksacks, fresh off the Malvern Hills, all clutching leaflets and books from the Tourist Information Centre.

"That's amazing!" said Emerald, "that Jean-Philippe may organise classes right here, just for you."

"It's not *what* you know," Tamsin enjoyed her last mouthful of cake, "It's *who* you know!"

Charity replaced her teacup on its saucer and gave Muffin a quick hug. "And if that doesn't work out, you can always ask Jeff. I'm sure he could suggest something."

"I'll ask Feargal to ask him. Where is Feargal anyway?" Tamsin peered round the café, as if their reporter friend might just materialise out of thin air.

"He's always in a rush," Charity said, gathering up her things. "That's why he's so thin. Never still. Just like young Freddie Benson."

"Freddie Benson?"

"He was at school with me. Never still. I can remember him falling off his chair on more than one occasion. He ended up as a shepherd. His sheep must have been nervous wrecks, I imagine." She smiled, with a faraway look in her eye.

"Maybe they calmed him down? He sounds like Alex - Chas's middle boy. He can never keep still."

"Lovely family that," Charity nodded firmly as she gave her

verdict. "And young Cameron is so good with their Buster. He reminds me of some Boys' Own type of story where the intrepid boy and his dog take on the world. He has such a bond with him ... Now you could take some lovely photos of the children, playing with the dogs! Perhaps at one of your Monday tricks classes in Nether Trotley?"

"There's a thought ... Know what? I'm looking forward to this now. And I can't wait! Jean-Philippe had better get this class going immediately."

" 'I want it and I want it now!' " laughed Emerald. "You have an idea and you expect it to happen straight away!"

"That seems to be the way I roll. And you must admit - it's worked up to now."

"True, dear. Once you get the bit between your teeth you're away!" Charity smiled maternally.

" .. with us just hanging onto your coat-tails." Emerald twisted in her chair and her face softened, "Talk of the devil - look who's just arrived!"

And Feargal, tall and gangly, strode through the café to their table, mouthing his coffee order to the pink-haired Kylie with a thank you smile, pulling out a chair and sweeping his auburn mop of curls from his eyes, all in a flurry of movement. And everything seemed right.

CHAPTER TWO

"Here - you can have my armchair, dear boy," Charity said as she fastened the lead to Muffin's harness and pushed on the arms of the chair to get up. "I have to go to the Library and I promised to drop in on Dorothy before I head back to Nether Trotley."

"Thank you Charity!" Feargal made a bow and picked up Charity's large and battered old bag, with knitting needles sticking out of the top, and passed it to her. "Good to see you looking on top of the world!"

"Flattery will get you everywhere," she grinned and allowed Muffin and Moonbeam a gentle nose-touch before proceeding through the café, greeting everyone as she went.

"She's a force of nature," sighed Tamsin as she sat back in her chair. "I hope when I get to her age I'm still as agile."

"Perhaps," Emerald looked pointedly at the empty plates on the table, "less cake now would help with that. I imagine Charity went through quite a lot of hardship in her day."

"You're quite right. I believe she did. Wasn't her father a farm labourer? They surely didn't make much. But there's little chance of me foregoing cake," she gazed fondly at her plate, then sat up straighter and said, "What's up with you this weather, Feargal?"

"Thought you'd never ask!" he said, accepting the mug of cappuccino from Kylie, along with two toasted sandwiches and a large slab of fruit cake glistening with glacé cherries, waving his card at her proffered machine. "The *Malvern Mercury* is reporting a few strange happenings, and I'm doing a bit of sniffing about."

"Oh yes?"

"Seems there's someone going round pinching unlikely things. Nothing of particular value. Doorknobs, car number-plates, pegs off a washing line - not the clothes, they were left in a damp heap on the grass, a road sign - you know with the name of the road on."

"Kids?" Tamsin suggested.

"Seems a bit too random for kids. The thefts are happening all over the Malverns. Great Malvern, Malvern Link, Malvern Wells, even Little Malvern had a lamp pinched off a gate-post. Nothing yet in West Malvern. So we're keeping our eyes open."

"What do the police say? Your mole must have some idea," Emerald stroked Banjo's grey and white head which was resting on her leg, his blue eyes flicking from one speaker to the next.

"They're baffled. Can't see a pattern. But they think it'll probably die out of its own accord. Somebody just being a nuisance."

"Can it be someone with a grudge against the victims?"

"Could be. But the thefts are pretty insignificant."

"Curious. What sort of mind would cook that up?"

"A malevolent faery!" Feargal sometimes betrayed his Irish heritage.

Tamsin laughed. "I'm thinking something a bit more rational. Perhaps someone's going to do something meaningful, and it'll be concealed in this stream of nonsense events?"

"Quite possible," Feargal nodded, absently shredding the serviette that had come with his coffee. "Nothing much can be done meanwhile. No forensics that they can find."

"Well, if that's the extent of crime in the Malverns at the moment, we can sleep safe in our beds!"

Emerald twirled her long blonde plait. "Pity Charity left. I bet she'd have an insight."

"Yeah - she'll have seen it all before ... somewhere in her long history. Let's ask her next time we see her." Tamsin turned back to Feargal. "So what else are you up to?"

"Cricket season has finished. No notable court reports - just the usual car thefts and pub brawls. It's down to 'back to school' stuff - I've got to do a piece on the new season of evening classes being offered .."

"Ooh - are there any photography classes?"

"Probably. You want to join one?"

"I do! Just to be able to take decent photos with my phone. Nothing fancy."

"I'll be having a look - I'll let you know. I see you've been admiring Jeff's pictures in the *Mercury*," he nodded towards the cream-spattered paper on the table, folded to display the picture spread. "He may be able to help."

Emerald leant forward, "But Jean-Philippe might organise a class here. Seems his Hereford friend in the underground coffee network," she grinned at the thought, "had some classes running."

"That would be perfect for you, Tamsin! But you'd smear butter icing all over the lens and get blurry pictures.," quipped Feargal.

"Haha. I can eat cake after. I'm not barmy!"

"And what about you two?" He asked. "How's your Autumn shaping up?"

"Just the usual yoga classes for me, mostly here in the upper room," answered Emerald. "But I'm getting more home visits, I'm happy to say."

Feargal smiled appreciatively at her as he munched his second sandwich.

"What about your meditation plans?" prompted Tamsin.

"Ooh yes! I'm going to offer meditation classes too - by popular request! I may do some sort of retreat towards Christmas. Got to work out how, though."

Feargal looked at her admiringly. "You're really developing your school! Must be rubbing off from Tamsin the business mogul, eh?" he smiled at Tamsin.

"Well, I'm getting really booked up for home visits too! I love doing them. And .. I've had a thought." She reached a hand down to Quiz's head for a little moral support.

Feargal raised a quizzical eyebrow.

"You know all the handouts I write to give to students - for homework and to remind them what I've taught them - well I'm thinking of making them into a book."

"Oh, what a brilliant idea!" Emerald clapped her hands together and Moonbeam gave a small woof. "Oh sorry, Moonbeam - didn't mean to startle you."

"Your monthly column in the *Mercury* certainly seems popular. You get quite a few comments, don't you?" asked Feargal.

"It is! And I do! I love writing it. So I may find out if I can add those pieces to the book too, or a version of them."

"Sure the Editor will sort that for you - especially if you give us a mention."

"It's still just an idea for now .. But I'd love to get this way of training out to a larger audience. Dogs deserve the best."

"Or, at the very least, kindness. Hey! You could add your own photos as illustrations, once you've learnt how to take good ones," Emerald enthused. There was a scraping of chairs as the hill-walking party got up from their tables, gathering their backpacks and walking poles, and tramped toward the door, their faces still wind-burnt and ruddy.

Tamsin suddenly sat up straight and looked at Jean-Philippe's clock on the wall - a curious clock with all the numbers in a jumble at the bottom and the hands pointing at empty space, presumably to lull patrons into a timeless visit - "Oh my! Look at the time! I must fly. I've got two one-on-ones today."

"What are they?" asked Emerald as Tamsin quickly assembled all her things.

"Um, the first one is a new puppy visit in Much Marcle. I do so love those - such fun transforming people from Sergeant-Majors to friends in under an hour. They can't believe how quickly I get results." She clipped leads to the three dogs and rolled up their mats, stuffing them into her capacious shoulder-bag. "And the next one is back in Poolbrook. Could be more of a challenge. The owners reckon their dog is defying them. 'Stubborn, wilful, plays deaf' - all the usual complaints."

"You'll soon bring them round," said Emerald, sliding her chair back to let the dogs pass.

"Say, Feargal," Tamsin paused and turned to her friend, "keep us up to speed over those queer thefts. I'm worried they may start stealing cake!" she laughed and waved a goodbye to Jean-Philippe and Kylie as she processed out of the café, her three dogs walking ahead of her like deerhounds.

CHAPTER THREE

"Your wish is everyone's command!" Charity smiled as she and Tamsin trudged up the steep slope of Midsummer Hill a couple of weeks later, their four dogs making light of the escarpment as they raced ahead of the two puffing humans. The sun still had plenty of heat in it, and as they ascended they could feel the light refreshing breeze strengthening. After the long dry summer the paths were yet to become muddy, so they were still able to walk in shoes, and leave the welly boots at home.

"So it seems. I was amazed how quickly Jean-Philippe got it all organised."

"And you start next Wednesday?" As they reached the top of the slope

Charity stopped and gazed at the marvellous view - as an excuse to regain her breath. It was a beautiful late September day. The mist had cleared and the greens of the trees and the fields beyond sparkled in the pale sunshine. The steep drop to their left revealed a small quarry lake shimmering in the light breeze, reflecting the blue of the sky.

"Yep. You saw those posters he put up, advertising photography classes?"

"I did. They were everywhere. But I think Feargal's mention of the course in his compendium of adult learning probably did the trick."

"It's fully booked anyway. It'll be fun to be a student again, and not have to worry about actually *running* a class. Here, Banjo!" she got her blue merle collie's attention and threw his beloved soft cloth frisbee. He thundered along below it as it wheeled through the air, leaping up to catch it at just the right moment.

"Banjo's so good at that!" said Charity, as Banjo ran back with his prize, holding it still for Tamsin to take, saying 'again, again' with his whole body.

"And the poor dog's got much better at it since I improved my throwing!" Tamsin took the frisbee and flung it again, this time watching it drift down the hill across the wind, her gallant dog racing after it.

"So what do you think you'll be doing at this class?"

"We've just been told to bring our phones, fully charged. And a notebook and pen. The first lesson is about composition, I believe. Should be good. I'm hoping it'll transform my photos!"

They walked on together in companionable silence, avoiding the areas of thick bracken, pausing to remove a bit of bramble from a bushy tail, or checking that the stick in a dog's mouth wasn't thorny or dangerous.

"Look at those blackberries!" Charity pulled a bag out of her pocket as she advanced towards a large expanse of brambles. Tamsin got out a bag too, and they both spent a while picking the juicy fruit. Quiz and Banjo picked their own, from lower down the bush, while the more energetic Muffin and Moonbeam played catch-me-if-you-can up and down the path.

Munching a particularly juicy berry, Quiz suddenly froze and stared into the bush. "Whatcha got, Quizzy? A mouse?" Tamsin stooped to peer through the briars to see what had caught Quiz's attention. The dog stayed stock still, her dark ears quivering slightly, her white mane bright against the undergrowth. "It's an old super-market bag .. seems to have something in it .. hope I'm not going to regret this!" she added as she stretched her arm out to capture the bag.

"Is it heavy?" asked Charity, as Tamsin dragged the bag free of all the thorns.

"Fairly heavy - it's got caught" she unhooked the briars from the side of the bag. "Here we are!" She gingerly opened the top of the bag and looked in.

"Whatever is it?"

Tamsin reached in and pulled out a door-handle. She held it up for Charity to see, then tried another lucky dip. "Can't pick this up," she grunted, then tipped the bag over and out rolled a stone ball.

"That's the top of someone's gatepost!" said Charity, turning the ball with her foot. "Look, that's the part that was cemented in."

"And what's this?" Tamsin poked through the autumn leaves and found the bolt off a door. "You know what this is!" she exclaimed, sitting back on her haunches and looking up at Charity. "It's the stuff someone's been pinching around the Malverns."

"Who the *Mercury* has named the Petty Pilferer! I think you're right, dear."

"We'd better make a note of this spot and take this to the police. There may be fingerprints or something."

"How are we going to mark this spot? It all looks so much the same." Charity looked around her. "I'm sure I'd never find this blackberry bush again," she puzzled.

"No problem! I'll use my phone! I can identify it on the map, give them the reference words."

"These phones are an utter marvel." Charity shook her head in wonder. "In my day you had to find a public phone box and be sure always to have two pennies with you."

"Did you not have a phone at home?"

"Oh no, dear. Only well-off people had phones. If it was a real emergency you could run to the Vicar's house and he'd let you ring the doctor. Otherwise it was the red telephone box outside The Cat and Barrel."

"The Cat and Barrel?"

"Long gone, sadly. Once Mike and Flo retired and moved to Dorset, to the seaside, there was nobody to take it over. Not enough people drinking in Nether Trotley. As the tractors took over, the farm labourers and the horse men became a thing of the past ..."

"You are a mine of information, Charity." Tamsin carefully stowed the objects back in the bag and started the slow walk back down to their cars. "So tell me, why would the Petty Pilferer be pinching these strange things, then hiding them under a bush on Midsummer Hill?" She checked her flock were all still with her and added. "Attention-seeking? Personal grudge against door furniture?"

Going down Midsummer Hill was a lot easier than coming up it. So Charity had breath to spare as they descended. "It reminds me .."

"Hoho! I wondered what you'd dredge up from your archives, Charity!"

"You may mock, dear, but it's sometimes useful, you know."

"Of course - and I wasn't mocking, only teasing. Go on ..."

"There was something not unlike this ... long time ago now. Bits were going missing. From the church, from farmyards, hitches off wagons - that kind of thing, even some weeds from someone's vegetable patch. Nothing of any value, just a bit of a nuisance."

"Here Banjo!" Tamsin floated the frisbee down towards the grassy area at the bottom of the hill, and watched with pleasure as her nimble dog leapt to catch it mid-flight, landed smoothly and circled back to her.

"It put people on their guard. Naturally if you have something taken, you think you've been targeted personally. People became uneasy. They started to doubt each other. Some of the schoolchildren decided to be the Famous Five and started hiding and snooping - it was a great way for them to enjoy the long hot summers we used to have back then."

Tamsin smiled as she remembered her own mother talking long-ingly about the long hot summer days of her childhood, with thunderstorms every night. People had wonderfully selective memories. But she didn't interrupt.

"Eventually the children caught the person in the act - they were lying in wait in a farmyard that hadn't yet been afflicted and raced to the Vicarage with huge excitement to tell all." She shifted her blackberry bag from one hand to the other. "It was old Millie Minchin. She'd always been a bit bats. Lived in a tatty old cottage that was crumbling round her ears. They found all the items she'd pinched in her henhouse, hidden under the straw in the nesting boxes."

"So why did she do it?"

"Nobody really knew. She denied it entirely. Ashamed, I believe. She spun some yarn about helping people. I don't know whether she had a Robin Hood complex and was trying to redistribute wealth in the village. Or whether someone had annoyed her one day, then she took all the other things to disguise the first theft? Don't they call it 'a cry for help' these days?"

Tamsin nodded, and collected the frisbee from Banjo, rolled it up and stuffed it in her back pocket. "What happened to her? Did the police do anything?"

"Oh goodness me, no! In a small village people would do their own policing wherever they could. They do stick together, you know - even the most unlikely and unpopular people are part of the village family. The Vicar would have talked to her, and would have tipped the wink to the doctor."

Tamsin nodded approvingly. "And I bet the kids thoroughly enjoyed their moment in the sun!"

"The schoolteacher talked to them about it. She was anxious that they shouldn't start persecuting poor Millie. And they didn't, to be fair."

"Did the stuff get returned to its owners?"

"Oh yes. One of the church ladies did that, so that Millie didn't have to."

"That all sounds very humane." Tamsin opened the back of the *Top Dogs* van and Quiz, Banjo and Moonbeam jumped in and settled down on their big bed. "Wonder what our present-day police would do? Can't imagine Chief Inspector Hawkins getting too bothered about a few missing doorknobs and some stolen clothes pegs."

"I'm sure they'd do much the same. Poor Millie was a few chicks short of a clutch. No point in making a big deal of it."

"So I wonder if a reincarnation of Millie Minchin is responsible for this lot?" She swung the heavy bag - which had got heavier and heavier as they walked - onto the floor of the van in front of the passenger seat.

"It's hard to know what someone like that is thinking. Hop in, Muffin!" Charity held her car door open.

"I'll drop this lot down to the station anyway, and give them the map reference. Over to them."

Charity got into her little blue car with Muffin curled up on the passenger seat, and wound down the window. "At least it's only a bag of swag you've found this time, Tamsin."

"And not a body! I know, I know. Let's keep it that way," she laughed carelessly as they both drew out of the tiny car park. "*Let's keep it that way,*" she repeated firmly to her dogs. But they didn't hear her, as they were already all asleep.

CHAPTER FOUR

Wednesday found Tamsin at The Cake Stop, filling up with coffee and cake before her first photography lesson. She had chosen a luscious caramel concoction with shards of toffee and lashings of whipped cream. She was surprised to find herself nervous, and had a sudden inkling of what it felt like to be one of her own students, turning up for their first class with their dog, in a strange place with a lot of strange people - wondering whether they'd make a fool of themselves, or be judged in some way. She decided immediately to spruce up her welcome speech, worrying less about herself and putting more focus on setting people at ease with each other, as well as with her.

"You are looking forward to your first class, *hein?*" asked Jean-Philippe as he tidied her table, one black eyebrow rising up his forehead.

"Oh yes, I am! Thank you so much for arranging it - just for me!"

"There are others, *tu comprends?* I see a few new faces here in the café this evening." He looked round his kingdom with pride.

"It'll be fascinating for me to have the boot on the other foot!"

"The boot? The foot? *Quoi?*"

"Being a student instead of a teacher for once."

"*Mais bien sûr!* It will be very different for you. Monsieur Barnstaple is already upstairs making the preparations. I will enjoy seeing your photos." He turned towards the door, "Ah look! It's Damaris Dodds. She told me she'd be coming."

Tamsin waved vigorously and called Damaris over. "Damaris! Are you joining the class too?"

Damaris - one of the three sisters known as The Three Furies because of their eccentric mother's choice of Ancient Greek names, and who supplied the most excellent cakes to The Cake Stop - hopped from one small foot to the other, clutching a scarlet tapestry bag up to her flat chest. She looks just like a Robin Redbreast, thought Tamsin to herself.

"Yes dear - so exciting! We need some better photographs of our cakes, so Penelope signed me up for the class. I do hope I can manage ..." she chewed her lip for a moment. "We'd like to be able to show off our icing skills when we do special occasion cakes."

"Absolutely! Your cakes are wonderful - and *of course* you'll manage!" Tamsin said as Damaris hopped again and twittered and blushed. "It's five to. I think it's time we went up," and she rose from her seat, looked about in puzzlement that all she had with her was her phone and a notebook, and no dog and training bag - she felt positively undressed! They headed towards the stairs to the upper room.

As they passed the counter they saw Kylie giving directions to the staircase to a couple of very thin women in their sixties, in walking gear. They nodded enthusiastically and nearly bumped into Tamsin and Damaris as they strode towards the stairs.

"Are you going to the photography class?" the shorter one demanded.

"We are! It's this way," Tamsin indicated the stairs and stood back to let them go first. They thundered up the staircase in their walking boots, their backpacks swinging behind them as they ascended.

"This should be interesting," she said very quietly to Damaris, who smiled conspiratorially back at her.

When they arrived upstairs, they found two rows of chairs facing a table bearing a slide projector, along with sheafs of paper, some large manila envelopes and three smartphones. Behind the table stood a nervous-looking man who seemed slightly puzzled at how he'd arrived there, but who beamed at the room in general and repeatedly said "Welcome, welcome, make yourself comfortable, do. Oh dear," his long artistic fingers fluttered as he spoke.

Oliver Barnstaple resembled nothing so much as an owl. His round gold spectacles and darting eyes, his bald dome with its fringe of long wavy light brown hair sticking out like a skirt round his head, along with his ancient brown tweed jacket, olive green woven tie, khaki-coloured shirt, shabby brown trousers and stout brown leather boots, gave him the appearance of the noble bird, if not a camouflaged bird-watcher. His fluttering hands completed the picture of fluttering feathers.

What a strange-looking person, thought Tamsin, and she wondered what her own students' first impressions were of her, and turned to more charitable thoughts about her new teacher. He flapped his wings and shuffled backwards and forwards saying "Oh dear, oh my good-ness," as his new students silently came in to the room.

The seats gradually filled as they filed in. Tamsin and Damaris sat at the far end of the second row, so she had a good view of everyone else as they arrived. The two hiking ladies elected to seat themselves right in the middle of the front row. Tamsin was surprised to see Mark Bendick from *Flying Pedals* parking his large self in the first seat at the other end of their row. She waved a hello to him, and watched as no sooner had he sat down but he had to stand to allow people to pass. Then he sat again - and had to rise again. Mark was not the sharpest tool in the box, she reminded herself, hence his continual falling by the wayside and getting into trouble with the law. But his mechanic job at the bike shop seemed to be the making of him. "Wonder what Mark wants to take pictures of?" She said to Damaris, who was riffling in her big red bag and too preoccupied to hear.

Eventually, all but one of the seats were filled, and the uneasy silence was broken by a violent throat-clearing from the teacher.

"Good evening everyone! You're very welcome. Um." He paused for a moment, remembered what he was doing and carried on. "I'm Oliver Barnstaple and I'll be taking you through this course to get great photos with your smartphone." He coughed again and laughed nervously. "You'll have seen from the curriculum you were sent, that I have a long experience in photography, and have embraced the advantages of the phones we all carry, which have some astonishing camera-power at their disposal. Knowing the technical side of photography is useful, but the best pictures come from knowing what you want as well as what your apparatus can do. Framing your image - that is to say, deciding what part of the object or view you want - is all-important."

Several people nodded sagely.

"I see from your enrolment forms that quite a few of you want to learn for a particular application. Let me see, er .." he shuffled some of the papers on the table around and went on, "Bicycles, action shots, cakes, dogs, plants, children, horses, landscapes .. hmm, quite a range. I hope to be able to guide all of you to getting the photos you want with much more confidence." He beamed at his audience, and some smiled back.

A thundering of feet on the staircase was followed by the door bursting open to reveal a flustered young woman with a mop of dark curls.

"Sorry I'm late!" She said breathlessly as she plunged onto the last remaining chair, bumping into people and scattering her bags round her. "Sorry! Sorry!"

Tamsin cast her eyes heavenwards. Some people never changed! It was Saffron, the young single mother who worked part-time at the local health shop, and who she'd come across when looking into the murder of Emerald's student.

Oliver nodded to her, frowned slightly, smiled, coughed, and continued. "Now, I need to take the register. Um, from now on you can just sign in as you arrive, but I want to put some faces to names, you know? So I'll actually take a photo of each of you as you call your name. I have a memory like a sieve, ha! ha!" he laughed apologetically, a strange staccato laugh. He picked up another sheet of paper and a pen, put them down again and waved his hands over the phones on his table before darting towards one and holding it up, pointing it at the rows of seats. "Joe Bucket?" he said expectantly, looking around his audience, and took a photo of the elderly man who waved his gnarled hand in response. He put down the phone, picked up the pen again and ticked off his name. "Mark Bandick?" "It's Bendick, sir," answered Mark politely, as his picture was taken and name corrected with much muttering of apologies, and ticked.

"Jessica? And Chloe?" the teacher peered into the room as if at sea.

Two teenage girls stood up languidly, twisting this way and that to give the photographer a pose to remember.

"Er, got it, thank you," muttered Oliver as he snapped a quick photo of each of them and ticked them off his list. "Now, let me see, just a few more ... Grace Metcalfe?"

"I'm here," a loud voice honked, and everyone turned to look at the brassy blonde woman wearing a polo shirt and a down gilet.

"Wonder what *she* wants to photograph?" said Tamsin very quietly to Damaris with a grin.

"Got to be horses, I'd say," whispered Damaris.

"Ah thank you. Um .. Ni-amh O'Connor?"

"Oh, that's me! Um, it's 'Neave'," the soft Irish lilt belonged to a mousy young woman who giggled nervously.

And so he continued getting everyone's pictures and names till he arrived at the last person - the taller walking lady in the front row, Janice Carruthers - who was identified and duly registered.

As a teacher, it turned out that Oliver Barnstaple was surprisingly effective. The time flew by as Tamsin listened intently to his slide presentation, explaining how to choose the best angle of a subject, and all the many things to consider in the composition before taking a shot. She found she had taken pages of notes and was just beginning to lose focus when Oliver said, "Let's have a brief break to stretch our legs. I'm afraid we only have water as refreshment, as the café downstairs meets our other needs. We've got through most of today's lesson, so, er, we can move about a bit before the last part." He busied himself with his papers in the hope that no-one would ask him any questions.

Tamsin was glad to get up and fetched herself and Damaris glasses of water. Bumping, literally, into Mark, who managed to slosh water down his front, she asked him whether he was the one wanting to photograph bicycles.

"Yes, that's me! I've been trying to capture action shots of the Nighthawks on their competition runs, and on their night-time sessions on the Hills, you know. Could do with a bit of help getting the focus right. They go so fast!" He laughed nervously.

"Is this for the bike shop?"

"That, and just for fun. I had a picture in the *Malvern Mercury* last year," he said with pride. "I want to get known for bike race photos. You're going to take pictures of dogs, yeah?"

"Too right! I need to get better photos for my posters and things."

"And your articles in the paper? Mum tells me she never misses them."

"Oh, that's good to hear!" She was impressed with how the awkward young man was beginning to really find himself in his new life at *Flying Pedals,* and gave him a genuine encouraging smile, thinking of what his mother Shirley - one of her students, who came to classes with the massive Pyrenean Luke - had had to go through while rearing this troublesome fledgling. She paused for a moment to listen to the two walking ladies behind her. One seemed to be arguing vociferously with the other.

"I told you this wouldn't suit us!" hissed the shorter of the two.

"I disagree," responded Janice Carruthers. "I've found it very useful so far."

"He's yet to show us how to take proper landscape photos." The first woman folded her arms in an impatient gesture.

"Give him a chance, Estelle! It's only the first lesson."

Tamsin's earwigging was stopped abruptly by a breathless Saffron, who greeted her as a long lost soul. "Tamsin! How lovely to see you!"

"And you Saffron. How's Charlie?" Tamsin would rather have

heard about how Saffron's yappy little dog Napoleon was doing, but remembered to get the priority right by asking about the baby first.

"Oh, he's wonderful, thanks! That's one of the reasons I'm here. Want to get some lovely photos of him. My phone is crammed with pictures of him already, but I want to make them better. Of course, I'm *really* here to improve my design photos for my business. Tax deductible!" she giggled, as she screwed up her eyes and raised her shoulders.

As Tamsin made her way back to her seat, she shook her head with wonder at what the hiking woman Estelle had been saying. What do people expect? Then she remembered that she should really know better! Some of her dog students expected a transformed animal within the first twenty minutes - and they always thought it was the dog that needed the classes, and not themselves.

"What are you chuckling at?" asked a lady with a round face, ruddy cheeks, a long pepper-and-salt pony tail, and a twinkle in her eye.

"Oh, just the waywardness of folk," Tamsin smiled back. "I'm Tamsin Kernick, and I want to learn how to photograph dogs."

The lady replied as prompted, "And I'm Lucinda Fry. I draw plants for horticultural books and want to improve my reference photos."

"That's fascinating! I'd love to hear more about that! I'm thinking of writing a book, and that's one of the reasons I want to be able to take better photos."

"Let's meet downstairs before the class next week, and compare notes!"

"Great idea Lucinda, I'll look forward to that. What do you think of our teacher?"

"Seems very able. I've learnt a lot already."

And so the lesson continued for a while longer till Oliver switched off the projector and faced them all as he leant on the table.

"There are handouts with some notes for you here," Oliver waved his large hand over a stack of papers. "Please help yourselves before you leave. There are assignments each week which I hope you'll enjoy and find useful. Do complete them, won't you! It'll make such a difference to your understanding, and indeed your progress. You'll see that you have to submit five photos to me for each assignment by email. I do hope you'll get to work together well. We'll actually be having some group activities. I suspect you'll be surprised how well these go." He rubbed his hands together and beamed once more at everyone. Several of the students rushed to the table to be sure of grabbing their handout, and the more forthright started bombarding him with questions.

"Good question, good question! Ah, you'll find a lot of answers in your notes there," he indicated the diminishing pile of handouts. "And everything else will come clear as we work through the course. Yes," he said, tilting his head back so he could peer down under his glasses, "that phone looks fine. Yes, I remember your question when you enrolled, er, Janice. We will, yes ..."

Tamsin took pity on him and quietly took her handout with a thank you and walked down the stairs. The café was now closed, the chrome and steel of the coffee machines glowing eerily in the half-dark, the room - normally so animated - still and quiet, with the lamplight shining through the front windows from the pavement outside, casting the shadow of the etched window signs onto the floor.

"The nights are drawing in," said Damaris ominously, as they emerged onto the cool, dark street.

"That means the end of my evening dog walks soon," agreed Tamsin sadly. She perked up and said, "Perhaps we'll learn how to take photos by moonlight!"

CHAPTER FIVE

"He's the funniest person, but he's actually really interesting," Tamsin was speaking through a mouthful of breakfast.

"And you've got homework?" asked Emerald, washing an apple.

"Yes! Haven't really looked at it yet. I took so many notes, but there'll be more to learn in the handout. Seems quite comprehensive. It's something to do with picking what you want to photograph then framing it."

"Deciding how you want it to look? So people don't have trees growing out of their heads?"

"That's the sort of thing! I'll work on that later. Have to brush my models first, won't I, kids?" she smiled at her three dogs who'd already had their breakfast and were waiting for some action. "You won't believe who else is in the class!"

Emerald quickly sat down at the table, agog with curiosity. "Who?!" she demanded.

"First of all, there's Damaris. Penelope sent her because she wants posh pictures of their posh cakes - you know, the special orders they do."

"That's nice!"

"Then I was surprised to see Mark Bendick there. He wants to make action shots of bike racers."

"It's so good how life has improved for him. You know, I think him getting involved in the hunt for the murderer of that cyclist has really brought out the best in him."

"Giving people responsibility often does, I've found. It's nice to know we make a difference."

"Who else do I know?"

"Oh! Saffron! She arrived late dropping things."

"No change there, then!"

"Bless her. She wants to take pictures of her darling Charlie, but officially she's learning how to present her business better."

"Good for her. Not easy being a single mum."

"And I met a really nice person called Lucinda. She's a kind of plant artist. Draws those super-accurate pictures of plants for textbooks. I'm meeting up with her before class next week. Oh," she waved her spoon as she swallowed her mouthful, "I took the bag Charity and I found to the police station yesterday too."

"Who did you talk to?"

"That nice sergeant. The patient one. He started teasing me. He said, 'Going down a notch in your detection, Ms Kernick? No bodies this time, just a bag of rubbish?' " She laughed as she scraped the last of the oats and raspberries from her bowl. "But he meant it kindly enough."

"I expect Inspector Hawkins will be glad you didn't bring in a body in that bag," Emerald crunched her apple.

Tamsin took her bowl to the sink. "But I did point out to the nice sergeant that one thing could lead to another, and who knew what this nut was going to do next?"

"What did he say to that?"

"Just carried on logging the details in his computer, with the map reference and all. He gave me a broad smile as he finished. It was a kind of Thanks-for-coming-hope-we-don't-see-you-again smile."

"It would be interesting to know who those things belonged to - why they were picked to be robbed, I mean."

"Ye-e-s. I don't know if anyone will tell us. But Feargal keeps his ear to the ground."

"And his snout to the molehill!" Emerald giggled.

"So I'm sure he'll tell us what he learns. Actually I haven't told him yet about this find. I'll do that now." She dried her hands, picked up her phone and tapped out a message to their reporter friend.

His reply came back fast.

I know

"Cheeky monkey! He's already on to it. I'd better not ever sign up to the Official Secrets Act as I obviously can keep nothing to myself!"

"I'm thinking of those people .." Emerald said thoughtfully. "Whatever reason this person has for gathering this strange collection of stuff - if they took something of mine I'd take it personally."

"So would I, come to think of it. I'd feel very uneasy. I'd wonder, 'Why me?' "

"So I'm wondering ... whether he - well he or she, I suppose - is actually targeting one particular person."

"And all the rest is a smokescreen? And it's not random lunacy? Only time will tell. Good thinking, Boy Wonder."

"*Girl* Wonder, if you don't mind." Emerald turned to the window and tossed her apple core out into the back garden. "Wonder who'll get that first?"

"It's a toss-up between the birds, the slugs, and Banjo. He loves apples. They clearly go well with all the bones he eats."

"It's so odd when people query you for feeding your dogs raw. What do they think dogs lived on for the last thirty thousand years since they joined forces with people?"

"And before that too! It's a sign of the times. Convenience food in plastic bags rules the world. It's what they eat themselves, so I guess they think their dog has to eat the same impoverished way." Tamsin reached down to rest a hand on Quiz's head, "Bet you're glad I'm not like them, aren't you Quiz?" A tail thumped on the bed.

"And I must say, since Opal started eating raw things - officially, I mean, she always ate raw things herself, being a good mouser - her coat's been so much stronger and shinier. Though she's such a madam, she still likes the cat stuff from the supermarket."

"It's a slow education. You should have seen what I used to eat before I arrived here from the Big Smoke!"

"Dread to think," smiled Emerald. "Which reminds me, you up for a trip to the Farmers' Market on Saturday morning?"

"Sure thing! We can stock up on *Hilda's Homebakes* as well as all the fruit and veg," Tamsin grinned.

"Ah well, got to get started." Emerald stretched languidly. "Got a private lesson to give, then I'm off to the Buddhist Temple for some meditation. Rounding off the day with class in The Cake Stop tonight."

"It's still a marvel to me that Great Malvern actually has its own Buddhist Temple. This is such a quirky place, between the townspeople, the scientists, and the hippies."

"Not forgetting all the creatives! This is why it's such a lovely place to live."

"And I'm going to sample the greatest benefit of all today - I'm taking my crowd up the Hills. Worcestershire Beacon today. I checked Stockwatch and there are no sheep there - they've moved them all up to the North Hill."

"Lazy day for you?"

"When will it ever be a lazy day for me?" Tamsin grinned. "I'll have a look at my photography homework over lunch, then I've got not one, but two, home visits to do."

"Anything interesting?" asked Emerald as she shouldered her yoga bag, one hand on the door handle and one stroking Opal on the end of the counter.

"Puppy chewing the owners to bits, and a dog who can't possibly do reward-based training because he doesn't like food. I wonder how he survives without eating anything?"

"Nothing new then," Emerald smiled as she gave Opal, stretching up to her with her eyes closed, a kiss on her tiny pale pink nose and went out of the back door, "See ya later!"

Once Emerald had gone, Tamsin decided to switch her schedule and work on her assignment first. Then she'd be able to do the work up on the Beacon - great excuse for staying there longer! So with pen and notebook to hand, she worked through the class handout and made some decisions.

It was a great day for a walk along the Malvern Hills. It was clear and sunny, with just a warm breeze and not the stiff cold winds that would nearly knock you over in a few months' time. Being September it was not too hot. The stunted trees and the bushes were beginning to lose their leaves, and small heaps were collecting in sheltered dips.

"Perfect!" she said to her dogs as they ran and snuffled and she walked. "But what's that?" Tamsin stopped to study an area of stripey grass going up the steep side of the Worcester Beacon, and as she got nearer, she saw an unusual sight.

Out of a dip appeared a team of two big horses hauling a heavy roller, followed by a stooping old man holding the long reins. The horses were magnificent - large, black with white blazes, with shaggy manes and feet, their complicated harness jingling as they walked towards her. Tamsin called the dogs in and put them on lead, just in case the horses spooked.

She watched as they approached, stepping easily through the taller plants. There was a pungent smell as the roller crushed the bracken, and she was pleased to see the driver, or ploughman, or roller-man, or whatever he was, slowly pull up as the horses reached her.

She recognised him straight away.

"Hey Joe! I met you at the photography class last night. I'm Tamsin."

"Oh, ahh, how-do, Miss." Joe took the opportunity to drop the reins, lift off his cap and mop his brow.

"I had no idea you did this! What *are* you doing, in fact?"

"Rolling the bracken. Has to be kept down. 'Tis poisonous to grazing beasts, so they woan't touch it. These Hills should be bare grass, not a forest of flaming bracken!"

"Flaming bracken .. it's the bracken that fed those wildfires a few years ago, wasn't it?"

"It were. You'm right."

"It's lovely to see the horses."

"Not many folk as knows how to drive 'em these days. 'Tis a dying art."

"Judging by those straight lines, it's an art you've mastered! I'm so pleased they're using horses. I'd have thought tractors would be much quicker."

"That's as may be. But tractors can't climb these steep hills. They'd tip over!" Joe laughed raucously. "And they'd get stuck in the dips and boggy bits. They do do some of the work, where it's flatter. But they can't do without us, can they, boys?" He rubbed the neck of one of the cobs fondly. "They'm not afraid of dogs. You can let your'n off if they don't nip their heels."

"Oh thanks! They're used to horses." She thought of her young friend Sara with her mare Crystal, who'd been instrumental in solving the bow-and-arrow murder in Bishop's Green. And she let the dogs loose again to their snuffling. They'd already sniffed their fill of the horses' heady scent while waiting and had catalogued them as not to be bothered with.

"So tell me, Joe, what brought you to the photography class?"

"I do be a gaarrrdener most of the time. Done some splendid gaarrrrdens in my time. I wants to get snaps of them to show people. Put them on the *interwebs*." He spoke the strange word with emphasis.

"I think a lot of us in that class are looking at improving our publicity for our businesses. That's what I want, with my dog photographs. I'm a dog trainer, you see."

"Ahh." He plucked a grass stalk and started chewing it ruminatively. "There do be a dog trainer who writes in the local paper. Talks some sense sometimes."

"That's me!" Tamsin laughed, and swelled with pride. "But I

mustn't hold you up. Hey, can I take some photos of you and what you're doing? It can be my homework for this week!"

"You do what you want," Joe adjusted his cap on his head, chucked aside his grass stalk, and posed next to his horses. Tamsin tried to remember everything she'd learnt and took a number of photos of the old man and his team. She looked at what she'd taken so far, realised the figures were getting lost in the background, and knelt down to capture the horses' black coats shining in the sunlight against the bright blue of the sky.

"Thank you, Joe! That's brilliant. I'll take some more once you're working again, if that's alright with you?"

"Ahh," said Joe, picking up the reins and walking back behind the roller.

"They never moved at all while you'd dropped the reins."

"Reckon as I left 'em in gear!" his wizened brown face cracked into a grin.

Tamsin beamed back. She'd warmed to this down-to-earth person who loved the land he worked on. "What will you be doing for your homework?" she called after him.

"Got a big Mongolia tree in a garden I'm working on. Going to consecrate on that for me photos. Good day to you Miss." He picked up the reins, spoke gently to his horses and they started slowly to walk on.

Tamsin watched them plodding steadily through the bracken, their harnesses creaking, the occasional snort as the dust rose from the drying bracken. She took a good few photos, positioning herself right on the lines with the horses ahead, then getting to the side and getting their silhouette against the North Hill. Hearing a mewing sound, she looked up into the wide blue sky and watched a buzzard wheeling on a thermal.

She sighed at the marvel of this paradise right next to her little town, and giving a shout to her three dogs, started the trek back.

CHAPTER SIX

Tamsin stowed all the shopping bags by their chairs in the window of The Cake Stop and settled Moonbeam on her mat, while Emerald carried over their coffees.

"Aahh," said Tamsin, stretching out her legs. "That's a welcome sight! I told Feargal we'd be here sometime, so he may crop up."

"I wonder if they've mentioned anything about your discovery, in the paper?"

"Didn't see anything yesterday. Here, who did you see at the Market? I had a chat with Hilda when I was filling my bag with her scones and doughnuts ..."

"I love the wholemeal bread from *The Crusty Loaf,* so I said hi to Malcolm. But he was busy explaining the sourdough process to some American tourists, so I left him to it. Saw you chinwagging with Jonathan though." She raised an enquiring eyebrow and pursed her lips.

"Yeah yeah. I was telling him how much my brother would love his cider, and how I'd be buying some from him for Christmas."

"I'll believe you, millions wouldn't," chuckled Emerald, who had the good sense to leave it at that.

"What I *did* see was Carmel on her *Sheep's Clothing* stall. She was fluttering around a customer helping them try on one of her Aran cardigans. So glad to see her doing well."

A cheery voice from behind their chairs heralded the arrival of their reporter friend.

"You kind of pop up from nowhere, Feargal," laughed Tamsin as she shuffled her chair across to make room for the chair he was pulling behind him from an empty table. "You're a sort of Scarlet Pimpernel."

"Better than a Ginger Pimpernel," he laughed as he swept his mop of auburn curls from his brow and got going with his toasted sandwich. "So why did I have to find out about your antics on the Hills from, shall we say, a third party?" he asked through a mouthful of ham and cheese, with a wink at Emerald.

"We have to make you work for your living, you know!" laughed Tamsin.

"Did they get any fingerprints?" Emerald asked.

"They got some partials, but so many that they can't do much till they have someone to check against."

"Mine'll be on there too. I didn't think when I picked up the first item. When I realised what it all was I was more careful. Any news your end?"

"Just that odd things are still going missing. Pump off a bicycle, concert poster off a lamp-post. And an rusty old bucket from someone's garden," he added, pushing away his empty plate and tossing his last crumb of toast to Moonbeam, who'd remained patiently on her mat knowing that Feargal would not forget her.

"It's all very odd," said Emerald thoughtfully. "It's either a nutcase, or someone with a grudge .. or someone wanting to hide a real crime in the midst of all this nonsense, as you suggested the other day, Tamsin."

"Let's hope the real crime isn't something nasty!"

"So how's your new venture going, Tamsin?" Feargal was already halfway through his lemon cheesecake and had started on his coffee.

"The photography class? Oh, I think it's very good. Strange old bird, Oliver Barnstaple. He actually makes me think of a brown owl.

But he seems to know his stuff. Here, I'll show you the pictures I took yesterday up on the Hills." She fished her phone out of her pocket and started tapping and swiping. "I happened to come across another of the students up there, at work with his horses." And she passed her phone over to her friends.

"Wow, those are terrific photos!" said Emerald admiringly.

"You'll be giving Jeff a run for his money with these shots," Feargal laughed. "I like how you've got them silhouetted against the bright blue sky in these two."

"You see, I've already learned a lot about what's behind the subject when framing a picture."

"And you're learning a new language to go with it!" laughed Emerald.

"You're right. We all have our own jargon, don't we? All your asanas, Emerald, and Feargal, you always say 'copy' when I'd say .. dunno, something else, anyway!" she smiled at him.

"But you actually talk normal English when you talk about dog training," he observed.

"You noticed! Yes, I do. I don't see the point of trying to blind them with science. I love it when students say, 'Oh, it's so obvious when you put it like that!' I actually want them to understand, so they can do better with their dog." She glanced down at Moonbeam, dozing on her mat in the shaft of sunshine coming through the window. "I think some trainers deliberately set out to look superior, rather than helpful, by going on about secondary reinforcers, and quadrants, and stuff like that. It's all science you have to know to be able to teach it right - but you don't have to inflict the strange language on people!"

"Sadly, I expect that's true - about other trainers," said Emerald. "I try to talk in normal language too. So my yoga students can relate, and not think they have to be having a spiritual experience every time they get on their mat."

"You both do well because you can relate to people," Feargal said thoughtfully, looking at both of them over his mug. "You back up your knowledge with an understanding of how people are - what stage they're at."

"Thank you, Feargal. And perhaps we should be working out what our clothes peg kleptomaniac is thinking. What's motivating them. Before something bad happens."

"*Mes amis*, you are talking about our mystery thief?" Jean-Philippe had materialised beside their table. "You may add something else to the list. I've just sent Kylie up to *Flying Pedals* to get her bike fixed before she rides home tonight in the dark."

"What's happened to it?"

"She just went out to the yard and noticed her rear mudguard was missing. Reflector gone."

"No! That's too bad."

Emerald said slowly, "How do you think they transport these things? I mean, a stone ball off a gatepost ... a mudguard - they'd be a bit awkward to carry about, wouldn't they? And Kylie's bike was interfered with in broad daylight!"

"That's a really good point. They must have a vehicle .."

"Or a very big pickpocket's overcoat!" laughed Feargal.

"I wonder ..." Tamsin said quietly.

"But I suppose it's only a nuisance, not dangerous," Emerald added.

"*C'est vrai.* But what is the Malvern Hills Detective doing to stop this nuisance, I ask myself?"

"We were just wondering why someone is doing this," Tamsin said, deciding to ignore the taunt from Jean-Philippe. "So far we have a kleptomaniac, a nutcase, someone with a grudge, or someone firing scattergun till he finds his mark."

"Or *her* mark?" A black gallic eyebrow rose up his face.

"Or her mark. Yes. That's possibly more likely," agreed Emerald.

"And I'm getting uneasy about it all." Tamsin sat back in her armchair and welcomed her little terrier onto her lap. After paddling her pointy feet for a moment, Moonbeam folded her long spindly legs under her and settled. "I can't help feeling there's something more serious going on."

"Or about to go on," added Feargal. "It does feel like something's brewing, yes."

"I only hope that whatever happens is as harmless as what's being stolen. But I'm not holding my breath."

Tamsin looked bleakly at her friends for a moment. Then she patted Moonbeam and said, "Let's get our shopping home and think about more uplifting things! A stroll across the Common will lift my spirits."

Emerald stood up and started assembling shopping bags. "With the timeless and wise Malvern Hills watching over us."

The four friends smiled. They had no idea how soon things were to change.

CHAPTER SEVEN

It was while Tamsin was returning to the *Top Dogs* van after a home visit in an old part of the town, that a thought struck her. She had no dogs walking with her and was thinking about the lesson she'd just been giving - to the owners of a very large, very hairy dog, who didn't seem to have bargained with the amount of shedding that would happen and were anxious to keep their new dog off the furniture. Apart from the training she gave the dog, she had spent some time explaining to the baffled owners about double coats and what tools were needed to keep them in order. And as she turned down a side road she heard a strange noise on the pavement of the road she'd left.

Dop, scrr, dop, scrr, dop, it went. Her curiosity aroused, she turned round and went back to the main road. And there it was. An old lady pulling a shopping trolley along behind her, one of those fabric bags on little wheels. It scraped along the paving stones and dropped into every crack between them. "Of course!" she said out loud, realising that this was the perfect way to smuggle stone balls and bicycle mudguards away, in plain sight.

The lady didn't hear her speak over the noise of her trolley as she trudged on up the hill - there were few places in Malvern that didn't involve a hill of some kind.

So we're looking for someone with a shopping trolley, she thought to herself. It would be easy for someone to stop their trolley where they intended their thieving and appear to re-arrange the contents while they secreted their stolen items. Far easier than carrying stuff along the pavement to the wide-open boot of a car. Got it! That's got to make it easier to find the culprit!

Then, as she reached her van near the supermarket car park, she realised her mistake. She could see at least four people leaving the shop pulling trolleys laden with shopping. She sighed.

Then she thought again. All the people she saw with trolleys were ladies of a certain age. No young man would dream of pulling such a vehicle, nor would any girls. She thought of Chloe and Jessica at the photography class and sniggered quietly at what they'd say if told to pull a shopping trolley. And women with children would have pushchairs or prams .. This *does* narrow it down, she thought triumphantly as she jumped into her car and greeted her patient dogs, who'd joined her for the ride.

"We're getting somewhere kiddos!" She turned and looked at them in their safety crates behind her. They all wagged their tails encouragingly. The only interpretation of that sentence must include the word 'walk'.

"Ok, ok, I know. We'll stop at the Common and have a scamper before going home to lunch. Don't know about you lot, but I'm starving!" And she put the van in gear and slid into the road.

The autumn weather was mild and pleasant. The chill of October hadn't yet arrived and it was still t-shirt weather for a lot of the day. On the Common they had been whacking more old bracken - this time no doubt with the tractor. The Hills were still a rich green above the town, the trees on the lower hillsides just beginning to turn yellow and red. She began to look at this view in a different way, thanks to Oliver's teaching, and she paused to take a few pictures from different angles - sometimes incorporating the trees in the foreground and sometimes focussing on the top of the Hills, amused to notice the 'hat' of cloud over the Worcestershire Beacon. Feeling pleased with herself she decided to spend some more time working on her photography after lunch. She had a good break till her Nether Trotley class this evening.

But this didn't stop the intrepid 'detective' from detecting. As she drove on home she looked at the houses and gardens she passed, and wondered what she would decide to steal if she had the addled brain of this trouble-making kleptomaniac. There was a little bit of round-topped metal fencing at the front of one garden - it looked as if the round bits could be removable, and some solar lights along the driveway in another. Doubtless there were some trowels and the like lying around on some lawns, along with children's toys, old flowerpots and the like. If this person was warming up to a theft of something valuable, what could it be?

One or two of the larger houses had carved stone signs bearing the house-name. There was a handsome pair of large bay trees in pots in a porch which must be worth something, and then her eyes lighted on the stone carving above the doorway. "I must walk around with my eyes shut," she confided to her dogs, now dozing as she drove home. "I've never seen that before! I wonder how many such things adorn houses in the Malverns?" And she wondered if this was the kind of thing the robber would target next.

Shelving all thoughts except those that involved food, she set about making her lunch. Some plaintive miaows caused her to capitulate and top up Opal's food bowl, and four big brown eyes (plus Banjo's two big blue eyes) bored into her soul till she did a quick bit of training with her dogs so they could earn some treats.

"This photo lark is getting absorbing," she told Quiz, who was sitting beside her in the garden as she ate her sandwich. And she started snapping off pictures of everything around her. She began to see the beauty in the different shapes and colours of her garden; the strong vibrant colours of the trees against the paler blue-ish shades of the Hills beyond them; the juxtaposition of different shapes in the bushes. And the buzzing of a bumble bee brought her over to photograph the flower it was feeding from. Disturbed, the bee buzzed away and flew over Moonbeam's head. Moonbeam knew all about the danger of snapping stripey insects and watched without moving.

Tamsin finished her lazy afternoon with more photos of her dogs, this time making sure to be aware of their surroundings as she chose her angles. She had a big selection to choose her five from, but eventually picked out her favourites to email to Oliver. "Time to prep for class," she announced, tossing her phone aside. "Nether Trotley tricks class this evening - you can come and show off, Banjo!" Thinking what a wonderful life she led, she added, "Thanks for being my inspiration."

She ruffled two hairy necks and one smooth slender one, and they all went indoors, the evening beginning to cool.

CHAPTER EIGHT

Wednesday afternoon, after a long phone call with a difficult client who liked to get her money's worth out of her private lessons, saw Tamsin eager and ready for her class, and she was looking forward to meeting up with Lucinda Fry beforehand in The Cake Stop. She was fascinated to learn more about what exactly Lucinda did, and how she earned a living from it. She saw that she was already at a table against the far wall. She snatched off her glasses as she saw Tamsin approaching the table, and stuffed them hastily in her bag.

"My treat," said Tamsin, as Lucinda came over to the counter to choose what she wanted."

"Oh, thank you, my dear! How very kind."

So, ensconced with their coffees and two tremendous helpings of carrot cake, adorned with little marzipan carrots - Kylie had made sure to add an extra one to Tamsin's plate - they started to find out more about each other.

Lucinda, who'd chosen a seat facing the door, was plump and rosy-cheeked - a homely, puddingy, sort of face - her long scraggy gunmetal-grey hair tied back in a low pony tail. She clearly enjoyed the good things in life and had no misgivings about tucking into her cake with gusto. To be fair, Tamsin didn't have many cake misgivings, but sometimes felt the weight of social disapproval and experienced guilt pangs.

And with her companion wading into her cake, Tamsin abandoned such feelings and joined in with equal enthusiasm. "How are you enjoying this program?" she asked between spicy mouthfuls.

"I think Oliver's really good - I'm already learning a lot."

"But you'd already know all about the art side, framing your image, and so on?"

"Yes, I'm good with composition. But it's the tech side I want. Lighting, avoiding reflections, close-ups without distortion, that kind of thing."

"Oh, I'd never thought of all that! I can see I've got a lot to learn. Tell me about your drawings."

"So I work mostly in coloured pencil," Lucinda was saying, "and occasionally in water-colour. The coloured pencil reproduces really well in book illustrations, and you can get very fine detail and gradations of colour."

"Not like the crayons I used at school, then?"

"Definitely not! They're premium artists' colours. I've got several hundred, all different shades. I sharpen them to a fine point for accurate detail. Precision's really important in my sort of work. Impressionism wouldn't do at all!"

"Wow. I had no idea! Ours came in a pack of six. No wonder I couldn't do much with them! Tell me the name of one of the books you've illustrated - I'd love to have a look." Tamsin put down her fork and enjoyed some of her coffee. "I think I told you, I'd love to write a book some time."

"You and about 80% of the population, apparently," laughed Lucinda kindly. "But it's like anything else really. You just decide to do it, then ... do it!"

"What a refreshing approach. After all, that's what I did with my dog training business. It was what I wanted to do, so I just learned what I needed and ... did it!" Tamsin gave a smug smile. "I'm gradually amassing the articles I write for the *Malvern Mercury*, so I'll have plenty of material to work from."

"And you'll be able to do your own illustrations once you've mastered photography of your dogs," Lucinda pointed out. "Ah look, our classmates are beginning to arrive. Who's that over there with Grace, the horsey person?"

"So she *is* horsey? I guessed as much."

"I've seen her out riding on the Hills, when I've been collecting photos and samples for my drawings."

"Are you allowed to pick things on the Hills?"

"The occasional frond of bracken, or leaf off a large tree, sure. I wouldn't dream of picking any flowers or pulling up a plant or anything like that. That's against the law, anyway," Lucinda nodded approvingly.

"I don't know who that is, the man that's with her. I saw him come in, and he clearly knows Grace. He looks a bit furtive to me, the way he's looking about."

"Hmm, you're right," Lucinda smiled and waved at Niamh O'Connor as the shy teacher slunk through the door. "Come and join us, Niamh," she called. Niamh blushed and scampered across like a frightened little mouse.

"Thank you," she said as she put her bag on the floor, her notebook on the table, and sat expectantly looking about her, her hands clasped between her knees. "Did you get your assignment done?"

Both Tamsin and Lucinda nodded. Niamh relaxed a little. "I had great fun photographing the children in the playground at lunchtime. Of course I can't *use* those photos for anything. I'd have to get parental permission. But I'm hoping it'll be alright to show Oliver?"

"I'm sure it would be ok," said Tamsin encouragingly, "so long as you're not publishing them anywhere."

"But I expect the parents would be only too pleased, once you ask them," Lucinda suggested.

"I'll have to get the Head to sort that. I must say, I had fun getting the right shots!"

"Here are the others." Lucinda finished her coffee and picked up her things as a crowd of people started up the stairs to the upper room. "Better go up!"

By the time they'd all signed themselves in, some of them giving friendly greetings to each other, and some still keeping themselves to themselves, the man who'd been sitting with Grace came up the stairs with her, spoke briefly to Oliver and took a seat.

"We have a new student to welcome this evening," said Oliver, after tapping the projector and getting everyone's attention. "Oh, umm, I'll just take a photo for my register ... It's Duncan Hattersley, isn't it," he said as he snapped a photo of his new student, who'd jumped to attention. "You make the class up to thirteen. Hope that isn't unlucky!" he beamed owlishly through his small round glasses.

"Yes, Duncan Hattersley," he gave an ingratiating smile to the room. "I'm documenting the architecture of the Malverns," he gave a nervous laugh. "Need all the help I can get!" he barked out and sat down abruptly.

The lesson began. Tonight's session involved a lot of technical information - comparisons between phones, editing software, and the like - and as some of the other students, Tamsin began to find her mind wandering. She amused herself by watching the others. Some were making copious notes in their notebooks. Damaris was nervously scribbling in hers, frowning and chewing her lip. Janice and Estelle Carruthers were sitting ramrod straight, listening intently. She saw the two girls Jessica and Chloe were on their phones, nudging each other, not paying any attention at all. She brought herself back to focus on what was being said. Tamsin decided not to take notes this time, but to rely on the detailed handouts which she could see ready for them on the desk. Oliver was illustrating his talk with examples, and it all started to make more sense when he demonstrated what he'd been explaining about light and lighting.

"I think this will all become easier with a bit of practice," he was finishing up his slide show. "And this week's assignment will give you plenty!" He cleared his throat. "Now, let's have a quick 5 minutes to stretch our legs, then we'll look at all the work you've submitted - great range of subject matter, I have to say .."

Tamsin made sure to snaffle her copy of the handout and walking back to her place with her focus on the sheet she bumped into Duncan Hattersley.

"Oh, I'm so sorry my dear," he said. "Must look where I'm going, haha! I was just, er, just .."

"Not at all. How are you finding the class?"

"Very good. Yes, very good," he nodded vigorously.

"And it's architecture you're interested in?"

"That's right. Fascinated by domestic architecture in particular. And Malvern boasts such a large range."

"Hope being Number Thirteen hasn't unnerved you!"

"I don't believe in luck," he suddenly turned serious. "I think we make our own luck. We are not the victims of circumstance." And so saying he turned on his heel and went back to his chair.

"What an extraordinary person!" said Saffron, who had chosen that moment to join Tamsin.

"Indeed! But I do agree with him," Tamsin replied. She had a shrewd suspicion that Saffron felt that she was the victim of circumstance rather than the author of her own downfall. When she found herself pregnant and abandoned she was unable to continue her interior design business and was seriously short of money till she got part-time work in the health shop.

So Tamsin changed the subject. "How's Napoleon doing?" Realising she'd got the priority wrong this time, she added quickly, "Charlie must enjoy playing with him!" And this opened the floodgates for Saffron to tell her all about Charlie's latest developmental milestones and wonderful achievements, which lasted till Oliver tapped the projector with his pen again to call the class back to order.

"Now for your assignments!" he said and with a flourish he magicked the first set of images onto the screen. They were clearly Mark's photos, showing cyclists hurtling down tracks. Oliver congratulated Mark on the way he'd captured the speed and excitement of the bikers. "You can see how what you've learnt today about lighting your image is going to help you with your next photos?"

Mark blushed that deep red reserved for men with sandy-coloured hair, folded his arms and sat proudly in his chair.

The next set of photos was rather unprepossessing, showing some slightly bleached-out images of cakes, clearly taken under the draining fluorescent lights in their modern kitchen. Damaris tilted her head and listened attentively as Oliver gave her some useful advice and referred her to the new handouts about lighting the subject. She nodded rapidly then tried to bury herself in her seat, making herself as small as possible - which was pretty small already.

It became clear who had taken which photos. Most of the students had chosen their pet subject. The two girls had taken lots of photos of themselves. You could clearly see their selfie ring-lights reflected in their eyes. Joe's late-flowering Magnolia tree looked resplendent in the sunlight. Some distant, rather dull, landscapes had been produced by both the Carruthers sisters. They showed views from the top of the Worcestershire Beacon. "You need to decide on what you want to achieve with this photo," Oliver explained gently. "Is it a topographical image? A misty, mystical picture? A contrast between the lowland farmsteads and the inhospitable mountains beyond?" Estelle tutted, while Janice bent her head over her notebook to jot down his words.

Lots of schoolchildren running around the school playground were clearly Niamh's. "Er, *Niamh.*" Oliver negotiated the strange name carefully. "You need to be a little more selective in your composition," Oliver told her. "At the moment this looks rather like an LS Lowry painting - which, of course, is fine in its way, but not really what I feel you are looking for here. You can still get the impression of lots of active energetic children running about while focussing on just a small section." He demonstrated by taking a couple of sheets of paper to the screen and showing where her image could be cropped. Niamh gulped and nodded silently, with a nervous smile.

Some studies of horses leaning over their loose box doors were clearly Grace's offering. They were pretty unprepossessing, and Oliver talked about depth of field and awareness of contrast, especially with the image of a black horse which was almost invisible against the dark interior of the box, leaving just his eyes glaring. "We'll be covering more of that in later lessons."

At last it came to Tamsin's pictures. She'd chosen a mixture, One of the creamy Opal stretched out in the sunshine by a clump of pale mauve autumn crocus, which brought some 'Awws' from the class. When she saw her dog pictures on the big screen she realised how they fell short of what she had imagined. But her portrait of the black horses against the brilliant blue sky drew praise from Oliver. He pointed out what she had done right, and looking intently at her over the top of his glasses, told her how impressive the image was. Tamsin was enthralled, grinned at Damaris who had turned to add her congratulations, and was so self-absorbed she missed the next few sets of photos entirely.

She caught up when she saw the horses again - this time in Joe Bucket's collection. He seemed to have a lot to learn still about composition.

Saffron's photos combined her first love - Charlie - with her business, by plonking the baby on the sofa she was photographing, having him on the floor next to a table, and so on. "Probably better if you didn't include the nappy basket and pile of dirty plates on the table," Oliver suggested, which brought shrieks of "Oh my *gosh!* I never noticed them!" from Saffron, clapping her hands to her cheeks.

"All in all, a very creditable set of first photos. I'm going to keep these, and we'll be able to measure your progress when we get to the last session." Oliver switched off the projector. "Now I have an announcement for you." He looked round the room to make sure everyone was listening. "Jean-Philippe has most kindly agreed to host an exhibition of our work at the end of this program."

There was an excited bustling in the class. Jessica and Chloe preened themselves in anticipation, while Damaris put her hand to her face, her mouth making a big 'O'.

"We'll have some photos downstairs, and more up here. So when the room is not in use, patrons will be able to come and view all the pictures. I'll be showing you how to mount your work later in the program, and hopefully you'll be happy to offer your work for sale."

A ripple of excitement ran through the class, which broke out into excited chatter and a round of applause before they gathered their things to leave. Niamh and Damaris started stacking the chairs, and Mark joined in, while Janice and Estelle buttonholed their teacher and started complaining that he hadn't said enough about their photos in his critique.

"You spent much more time on those pictures of bikes," accused Estelle scornfully.

"And the close-ups of plants," added Janice.

"And the horses. I wanted you to talk more about *my* pictures."

Oliver Barnstaple hesitated for a moment, then clasped his hands together in front of him. "It's always my intention to offer the help that's needed at a time when it will be received. The last thing I want to do is put someone down and spoil their enthusiasm." He raised his hands in front of him as Estelle drew breath for another salvo. "I can assure you your photos will improve dramatically over the weeks."

Janice folded her arms with a flourish.

"I think you'll benefit a lot from this week's assignment, which is designed to take you out of your comfort zone. Yes?" he turned to Duncan, who was waiting patiently by the desk. "You want last week's handout? Of course, let me see ..." He went to his case and riffled through the contents at length. By the time he'd drawn this process out as long as he could and located the handout for his new student, the grumpy women had left.

Tamsin, who had been chatting to Lucinda and Damaris, observed all this. "There's always someone," she said quietly as she nodded at the retreating backs of the indomitable ladies as they went out of the door, their angry footsteps thumping down the stairs.

CHAPTER NINE

"Hold it, Quiz!" The big dog looked up soulfully into Tamsin's eyes as she clung on to the metal spoon, her teeth chattering slightly against it. "Good girl," Tamsin coaxed, as she gradually settled into holding it firm and steady.

"Whatcher doing?" asked Emerald, looking up from her book which was propped on the cat on her lap, her legs folded beneath her on the sofa.

"Quiz has never been that good at holding metal. I didn't know it was hard for them and Quiz is my first dog. So she got all the mistakes!"

"So you're catching up?"

"Yep. I teach them to play with teaspoons and other metal objects when they're puppies now, so Banjo and Moonbeam have no trouble at all with metal."

"And that's useful?"

"Ooh yes - you never know when they may need to find my car keys for me!"

"I know Moonbeam always brings us the tv remote when we drop it - I suppose that's hard to pick up too."

"Hard and smooth and difficult to grip, yes." Tamsin beamed at

Quiz, who had held, then released, the spoon several times during this conversation, getting a morsel of cheese each time as reward. "Not to mention, delicate!"

"Hey! That's clever!" Emerald said excitedly, as she watched Tamsin place a cube of cheese in the bowl of the spoon while Quiz carried on holding it. "Clever girl!" said Tamsin, "Give," and taking the spoon she turned it so Quiz could eat the cheese.

"Yeah, I thought it may make a cute photo - to have each of them holding something."

"It sure would! Do you think of photos all the time now?"

"It's certainly given me a new way to look at the world." Tamsin ruffled Quiz's neck and leant back in her seat. "I suppose this must be the way artists see. Everything is light and shade and form. Like," she turned to the bay window, "they wouldn't just see a window, they'd see ... um, actually, I'm not sure what they'd see! I'm just a beginner."

"I get you. They'd see colours and contrasts, hard and soft, dark and light, I imagine ... that's really interesting. Think I'll have to start looking at things differently," replied Emerald, snapping her book shut, making Banjo twitch in his sleep, and tossing her long blonde plait over her shoulder. "So what's your assignment this week?" she asked as she started gently massaging Opal's ears. The cat lifted her head, nose up, eyes closed, and purred quietly.

"We have to make images which represent Malvern as a country town. It's not really a market town, of course - it's a spa town. But it plays the part of a market town."

"That should be easy for the new bloke you mentioned, the one who's into architecture?"

"I think we're meant to be capturing the essence of the life of the town, rather than its buildings. So I'm going to have a go at the Farmers' Market on Saturday."

"And today? Got time between sessions for some snapping?"

"I'll make time! I've got a home visit in Madresfield later this morning, so I'm going to go to the shopping centre while I'm out that way and catch the modern aspect of supermarket shopping. Then I'll wander up to the Elgar steps and capture some of the older types of shop."

"You're quite taken with this, aren't you, Tamsin!"

"I am! And you know how I enjoy meeting another strange group of people," she laughed.

"And they sure are strange, by all accounts."

"Shy, angry, bashful, grumpy, brash, dozy ..."

"Sounds like the seven dwarfs!"

"Hi-ho!" Tamsin sang. "It's off to work I go!" and jumping up from her armchair she cleared their coffee mugs and went out to the kitchen to get her work things ready, whistling merrily. "Coming, Moonbeam? It's your turn."

So after helping the old lady in Madresfield, showing her how to manage her dog so that he had better things to do than chew the furniture, she and Moonbeam went to the shopping centre for her first photoshoot.

She concentrated on the assignment, aiming to capture the impersonal vastness of the car park, the industrial lighting and signage everywhere, and the people intent on pushing their noisy metal trolleys, laden with shopping bags. Attaching Moonbeam's lead to her belt so that she wouldn't jog her arm in the middle of a photo, she set about finding unusual angles. She gave a cheery wave to one or two of her students doing their weekly shop - slightly bemused to see their dog trainer crouching beside a bin, angling her phone upwards, squinting into the sun. It was one of the pleasures of her work that she got to know so many people. Some of her early clients were already coming back with a second or third dog. She also saw the black curly head of Saffron, who was managing to push her trolley, baby Charlie in the seat, into other people, apologising as she went. Tamsin sighed, smiled, and shook her head.

"It'll be quite a contrast in the old part of the town," she said to Moonbeam, as she hopped her into the passenger seat of the *Top Dogs* van. "Here," she said, attaching the little dog's harness to the seatbelt, "you can ride shotgun for once!" and they set off up the hill. And who should she see on her way, but Jessica and Chloe. They were posing for each other outside one of the fashion shops, mimicking the mannequins in the big shop windows. "I suppose that's their representation of Malvern - how they see the town!" she thought, as she drove past. They were far too pre-occupied to notice her wave.

Finding somewhere to park the van, she made her way, her little dog by her side, to the Elgar statue at the top of the town. The composer Elgar gazed down Church Street from his vantage point on Bellevue Island, and Tamsin sat at his feet to capture the comings and goings of people about town.

It was a warm and pleasant day - the town was busy, the pavements fairly full, and as she chose which areas to photograph, she noticed a figure wearing a headscarf scurrying down the hill, pulling a shopping trolley behind her. The shape of her shoulders was familiar ... of course! It was Estelle. Tamsin usually sat behind her in class, and her characteristic bony shoulders were easy to recognise. She snapped off a few photos. Then she panned over to the other side of the street, and spotted the new student, Duncan. He was standing in a dark doorway, and yes! he was definitely watching Estelle. But as she turned off down a passageway trailing her trolley behind her, he slid out from his hiding-place and walked away down the hill, pausing to take a quick photo here and there.

"Curious!" Tamsin said to Moonbeam, and continued busily taking photos. "I wish I had your ability to spot things - I bet you can see a lot more than me. Dogs are good at seeing movement." Moonbeam obligingly wagged her tail.

"But one thing you can't do is rewind!" she smiled as she stood up and slid her phone into her pocket. "I'm going to take a closer look at all these photos when I get home. I wonder what I may discover ... And you know what, Moonbeam?" Her little dog looked up expectantly as she trotted along beside her. "We're going to make a detour to The Cake Stop to see your public! I don't have any more appointments today, and all this concentration has given me an appetite."

It was only after a delicious flat white coffee, and an equally delicious slice of light Victoria sponge - one of the Furies' specials, with their own strawberry jam and mounds of whipped cream - and a long leisurely chat with Kylie and Jean-Philippe about nothing in particular beyond learning that Kylie's bike was once more roadworthy, that Tamsin stretched her legs and set off home with Moonbeam.

Once home she looked over her photos again, frowning as she did so. She turned to all three dogs, tapped the phone and said, "You know what? I'm going to get a bit of help."

She pressed a button and was soon hearing her friend Feargal's voice. He sounded busy, the clatter of the office in the background. "Got a job for you," she said. "Can you find out anything about a couple of people? One is Duncan Hattersley. Middle-aged, guess he lives in Malvern. And he has a friend, Grace Metcalfe, horsey individual."

"Something fishy about them?"

"I think so, definitely."

"Ok," said Feargal hurriedly. "I'll do it later. It's all systems go here - there's been an unexplained death."

CHAPTER TEN

"An unexplained death?" Emerald was aghast when she arrived home from giving her yoga class at The Cake Stop that evening. She dropped her yoga bag at the foot of the stairs and peeled off her turquoise jacket, hanging it on the newel post.

"Apparently. And you're not going to believe who it is!"

"Oh, please not someone I know," wailed Emerald, scooping up Opal and clutching her close.

"No, not someone *you* know. But someone *I* know. Slightly."

"Go on then! Don't spin it out!"

"It's Estelle Carruthers, the grumpy woman from my photography class!"

"NO!" Emerald's responses were most gratifying.

"They found her in the car park at the bottom of Midsummer Hill. No car - seems she must have been taken there."

"Oh, that sounds nasty. What did they do to her?"

"Bang on the back of the head. But, hear this - she was lying by a big stone, you know those big boulders they use to border the car parks round here? So she may have fallen backwards onto it."

"An accident?"

"Could have been. The details are a bit sketchy at the moment ..." Tamsin was interrupted by a hullabaloo of barking. "Ah, this'll be Feargal now!" She got up and pacified the dogs by telling them, "It's Feargal! It's your friend Feargal!" and opened the back door for him. "Come in, come in, have you eaten?"

"Does it matter whether I've eaten or not?" he said with a cheeky grin. "I'm always hungry anyway!"

Emerald was already by the kettle, getting mugs ready, and Tamsin magicked up some cheese and biscuits and a few grapes, while Feargal did his 'long-lost-sailor' act with the dogs as they bounced excitedly round their special friend.

They got themselves organised with mugs and plates and bowls and retired to the living room to sit in the comfy chairs. Quiz chose her big squashy bed to lie on, while Moonbeam selected the space next to Opal on the sofa, and Banjo - in hope of a game - sat in front of Feargal with a soft toy in his mouth.

"Banjo, find your ball on a string. We're eating now." The blue merle collie turned and looked sadly at Tamsin, and nudged the toy onto Feargal's knee in a last-ditch attempt at a game.

"Later, Banjo. Promise!" said Feargal as he put the toy beside him on the chair. "I'm eating now." He pointed to his plate.

Banjo wandered over to a space on the hard floor and threw himself down with a big sigh next to a comfy dog bed.

"Go on then," said Tamsin, seeing that Feargal had almost cleared his plate while she was still just sitting down.

"Victim: Estelle Carruthers. Place: Midsummer Hill Car Park. Time of death, early evening. Cause of death: blow to the back of the head. Dunno if there's anything else - we'll have to wait for the post mortem results." He ate the last chunk of cheese, and looked regretfully at the grapes. "Want these?" he asked Emerald, on the sofa with Opal. "I know I'm not allowed to let grapes anywhere near dogs."

"You have the important things in life well sorted," said Tamsin approvingly, as Emerald took the sprig of grapes and Feargal put his plate on the floor.

"Things to note: there was no car in the car park. How did she get there? Too far to walk from her place down the bottom of Malvern Link. No immediately obvious signs of force, like bruised wrists or broken nails, so she must have known her attacker."

"Definitely an attacker?" asked Emerald. "I mean, maybe she went up with someone and there was this accident and they panicked and ran away?"

"Or she could have been dropped off there by someone and tripped and fell while waiting for someone else?" Tamsin put in. "Though she was pretty fit, it seems. Lots of hill-walking. Not likely to trip over her own feet."

"We haven't had much rain recently, and the car park is on hardened ground. But they're having a go looking for tyre tracks. See if they can identify any cars. Of course there aren't any police cameras out that way."

"Not many cars go there. It's a nice deserted Hill, most of the time, which is why I like it!" Tamsin agreed. "There's the earthworks of the ancient hill fort at the top, but not many people know about that. It was good fortune someone found her so quickly."

"Any other useful clues left lying around?" asked Emerald.

"They're doing the usual comb of the area, but nothing so far. Now, come clean, Tamsin! What's your connection?"

"Very little connection really. She happened to be in the same photography class as me. With her sister, Janice. Wow, she's going to be devastated - they seemed to be inseparable. Long hill walks and the like. Don't believe either was ever married." Tamsin finished her last grape, and putting her plate on the floor, patted her lap for Moonbeam to jump up and arrange her long thin legs on. "She seemed to be very tetchy. Always complaining to the teacher about one thing or another."

"Perhaps someone had had enough of her bad temper."

"Possible. But there's something else ..."

Two faces looked expectantly at her.

"These mysterious robberies. I was thinking .."

"Always a bad sign!" laughed Emerald.

"I was thinking," Tamsin repeated in a snooty voice, but with a smirk, "that a really easy way to spirit these things away without being seen would be to use a shopping trolley."

"From the supermarket?" asked Feargal.

"No, no - those little fabric bag things on tiddly wheels. Used by ladies of a certain age."

"Ah yes," he nodded.

"It would be much easier to move around unnoticed, rather than carrying things to a car. And you could have the trolley right with you as you pilfered."

"You're right - that makes sense."

"And nobody notices a woman pulling a shopping trolley behind her. They wouldn't even see her! I found that out after I'd had the idea and then I saw them everywhere!"

" 'A monstrous regiment of women'. Who was it who said that?" asked Feargal.

"Didn't you pay attention in history lessons?" teased Emerald. "It was some Protestant church guy a few centuries back who disapproved of Queen Mary."

"Because she was a woman?"

"Nah, because she was a Catholic. He just used her gender as an excuse."

"Misogyny was more acceptable than papism in those days!" Feargal observed.

"Still is, for some people!" she sighed.

"But you're right, a regiment. They're everywhere," Tamsin agreed, "little old ladies and some not-so-old ladies pulling their rattly trolleys along behind them."

"Excellent camouflage," Feargal nodded.

"And then ... "

They looked expectantly at her again.

"I was doing my photography homework - capturing the activity in Malvern - and I saw her."

"Who?"

"Estelle. I could only see the back of her and she was a fair way down the hill, but she sits in front of me at class and has very characteristic shoulders and a marching gait. She was pulling one of those trolleys behind her."

Emerald gaped gratifyingly. But Feargal said, "Hardly conclusive evidence."

"True. But a bit of a coincidence, wouldn't you say? That someone who *may* have been doing all these thefts just happens to find herself dead?"

CHAPTER ELEVEN

Emerald was off at one of her meditation sessions at the Buddhist Temple in Great Malvern on Friday, and Tamsin took the opportunity to go through her pictures from the day before.

She picked a few she thought would do for her assignment. She was pleased with the contrast she'd shown between the modern shopping centre and the traditional shops in the town. And she noted the calmer air of the town photos, with people acknowledging each other and stopping to chat, while at the supermarket they all seemed to be on a laser-focussed mission and hardly saw each other as they raced past. She cropped one or two of the pictures to emphasise this. "There'll be a big contrast when I add in the Farmers' Market photos tomorrow - it's a completely different vibe," she assured Opal, who was lying stretched out on the table in front of her where she'd found a square of sunlight - a yard of cat. Opal didn't even twitch a whisker at this exciting information.

Tamsin zoomed in to study some of the town photos. There was Estelle - on one of her last journeys - pulling that trolley along behind her. She looked again at Duncan in the dark doorway, watching. She scrolled through a few more shots, taken in quick succession. "Hang on!" she said sharply, causing Quiz to lift her head from her doze. "What have we here?"

Zooming in further and peering at the images, she could see her new friend Lucinda, looking into a shop window. Then the next frame showed her looking in Estelle's direction. She could be seen clearly sliding something into her handbag, looking about her furtively, then stepping away from the shop and following Estelle.

Tamsin scrolled a bit further through the pictures. Yes! Lucinda was turning into the same lane that Estelle had gone down. She leant back in her chair and sighed. She'd liked Lucinda. Could she be implicated in some way in Estelle's death? She bit her lip. "I really hope not, guys."

The only response was from Moonbeam, who got up, turned round twice, and lay back down in her donut bed again, snuggling her chin into it.

There were a few more photos to look through, taken earlier in the sequence. There was Duncan Hattersley, walking up Church Street. And - there was a brassy blonde head a little further down the road, heading away. It was Grace Metcalfe! They must have just passed. Were they talking to each other? They seemed to know each other, so nothing odd about that! Or was there?

Tamsin sat back and gazed out of the window. It was a bright day and some early autumn leaves were fluttering down in the breeze. "Am I seeing things that aren't there?" she asked Banjo, who'd come over dangling a knotted sock from his mouth to check whether her movement meant a game might be forthcoming. "Am I getting darkly suspicious about everyone?"

She looked into his clear blue eyes, gazing up at her. "This is how we fixed it in the other cases," she told him. "We don't have fingerprints and DNA and all that stuff that Hawkins relies on. We just have our thoughts and feelings." She ruffled his head. "And my present thoughts and feelings are telling me that something is going on here, Banjo

Bunny." He rested his chin on her leg. "And I'm also thinking it's time to get up and move - come on!" and she jumped up and led the way to the garden door, hotly pursued by three dogs who had instantly sprung to life and were ready to enjoy some fun.

She had a few games of fetch, and, noticing her shoes were getting wet from the rather long grass, she wondered whose turn it was to mow the lawn. Won't be long now before we can stop that for the winter, she thought, and looked up at the Malvern Hills above her. She could see a couple of tiny figures walking along the path on the crest of the hill, up to the Worcestershire Beacon, and suddenly felt anger surge up within her.

Estelle wouldn't be seeing the winter. She wouldn't be enjoying the cycle of the seasons any more. She would never again walk up the Worcester Beacon. No, she wasn't a very nice person, but that was no reason to cut her life short. Even not-very-nice people had a right to their lives.

Tamsin felt the flame of justice burning inside her. She had to do something about this! She stomped back into the house and grabbed her phone.

"Feargal!" she said, as he answered. "Did you find anything out about those two names I gave you?"

"There was a snarl-up on the Hereford Road this morning - a lorry cornered too fast and shed its load. It's the second time the same company have fallen foul of the law, so I've been busy doing a bit of investigation into that, sorry."

"Ok. But can you check them out?"

"What's eating you about them? I can' hear your nose twitching from here!"

"I was taking photos in town yesterday -"

"I'll have to warn Jeff to look to his laurels, that you're coming after his job at the *Mercury!*"

"You jest. But I may have something here. It wasn't that long before Estelle's last trip to Midsummer. I told you I saw her pulling that trolley in town around lunchtime yesterday? Well I've been looking more closely at all the photos, and I've also spotted Duncan Hattersley lurking in a doorway watching her."

"Oh?"

"And shortly before that he'd possibly been talking to Grace Metcalfe."

"You're doing well with circumstantial evidence so far. Got anything more concrete?"

Tamsin slumped back in her chair. "No. Just a gut feeling."

"Your gut feelings are legendary!" Feargal's normally mellifluous voice came thinly out of the phone. "That's enough for me. I'm on it!"

"Great! Thanks! Hey - any news? Your mole been squeaking?" Tamsin and Emerald were always teasing Feargal about his very useful contact in the police station.

"A few squeaks. But they haven't got much yet. They didn't find anything more at the car park, and they're waiting for the PM. So rather in the doldrums at the moment. It seems the victim's sister broke down dramatically when they gave her the news."

"Poor Janice. She must be shattered."

"But remember how many murders are committed within families?"

"You're right. I should be looking at her too. I've got my puppy class this afternoon, but I'm going for a long walk up the Hills now - this weather is so lovely. And the breeze will be fresh up there - clear my head."

"Ok, kiddo. You doing any more spying?" Feargal chuckled.

"I am! Tomorrow I'm going to be taking photos at the Farmers' Market in town. It's part of my assignment for this week. I may see some of the other students there too. Some of them work during the week and will be doing their project work at the weekend."

"Glad to hear someone works for their living," laughed Feargal. Tamsin decided not to rise to the bait.

"I'll take millions of pictures, and we can study them over the weekend."

"Sounds good to me. Jean-Philippe's, Saturday afternoon?"

"Perfect. See ya later, alligator."

"You come from a previous age. I will decline to understand that phrase," Feargal quipped as he rang off, leaving Tamsin smiling fondly at his image on her phone screen.

CHAPTER TWELVE

"So is this a shopping trip, a photography exercise, or is Tamsin the Malvern Hills Detective on the case?" asked Emerald, as she walked into town with Tamsin and Quiz the next day, shortening her usual long strides to accommodate her companions.

"Haha! I'm glad to see you have the shopping bags. I want to take a bit of a detour through Priory Park. It's a lovely Autumn day and there may be plenty of people there for photos." She looked up at the bright sky, with little clouds scudding across. "And as for being on the case ... well, we have to do what we can, don't we."

"I suppose you're right. When I started out giving yoga classes, I never thought I'd end up with a mad dog-lady who collected dead bodies like they were stamps."

Tamsin laughed loudly. "Mad dog-lady! Love it. So does Quiz, don't you, girl?" she smiled fondly at the big dog walking between them. "Do people still collect stamps? Don't worry, I'll help with the shopping too. But it would be good if you could grab some of the best fruit and veg while I'm taking photos."

"And interviewing suspects?"

"I only know the people in the photography class who knew

Estelle. I don't know her whole history. And who knows who may have got upset about her thievery and decided on a bit of rough justice?"

"But you have all these people going round town taking photos. Perhaps someone else took some on Thursday? Maybe there's more evidence to be revealed at your class next week?"

"That's a point. Hmm. We'll see who was taking pictures in town that day and I can talk to them then. Here, do you want to go straight on to the Market? I'm turning off here for Priory Park."

And so they went their separate ways. There were a good few folk in the park - mothers with pushchairs sitting round the hundred-year old ornamental bandstand, having a natter while their toddlers played; a trio of old ladies admiring the late summer flowers; and ... Joe Bucket! He was staring with a puzzled expression at the screen of his mobile phone.

"Hi Joe, you doing your homework?" Tamsin said cheerily.

"That I am. 'ere, didn't you have a few dogs last time I seen you?"

"I did - just bringing one out with me today. This is Quiz."

"Morning Quiz," the old man said obligingly, and patted her on the head with a brown gnarled hand. "I'm just taking pictures of these gardens. After all, 'tis gardens I want to learn how to take pictures of."

"That makes sense. Got some good images to show off next week?"

"I got down on me knees and took a photo of that there bandstand through the stone balustrade over there."

"Oh, that sounds good! Framing your picture in more ways than one. There are some magnificent trees here, aren't there."

"So there are, so there are," he nodded appreciatively. "Course I'd rather take pictures without them people in. But Sir says we'm got to have people, so that's what Sir's gettin'."

Tamsin smiled. She liked this old man, and if she ever needed anything done in the garden, she'd know where to go. "Seen anyone else from the class?"

"Yer. Saw that flibberdyjibbet with the curly hair racing around taking photos up by the Priory."

Tamsin nodded and smiled as she recognised the colourful description of Saffron.

"And I can't go anywheres without seeing them two gels posing like summat out of a magazine."

"Jessica and Chloe? Yes, they're funny, aren't they! I'm off to take some photos at the Farmers' Market and see if there are any late strawberries."

"I've got some boo'ful raspberries on my allotment. Want to drop over and get some, Miss? I can't eat 'em all!" Joe showed all his uneven teeth as he grinned. "I does have a table for them, with a box for you to leave some money in."

"I'd love that! Thank you Joe." And they arranged a good time for her to drop by in the week to have a good chance of getting some. She hurried on to the Market, being sure to pause and take some photos of the Market framed by the fifteenth-century Abbey Gateway. The green and white striped stalls shimmered in the bright sunshine, their table coverings flapping in the breeze. It was busy, and noisy too, with the musicians playing their tabors and sackbuts, their jesters' hats covered with bells adding to the lively atmosphere as they bobbed and pranced.

When it came to choosing compositions for her photos, Tamsin was spoilt for choice. So she took photos of the lovely array of baked goods at *Hilda's Homebakes,* then the bright colours of the different fruits and vegetables on Gary's stall, being careful to include some shoppers pointing to what they wanted to buy. 'Sir says we'm got to have people,' she reminded herself with a smile. Carmel's *Sheep's Clothing* stall had some long hand-knitted socks dangling from the top, moving prettily in the light wind, with Carmel below them knitting something very colourful. And the sun darting in and out of the clouds made lovely reflections on the dark bottles on Jonathan's *Cider Flagon* stall. She gave him a cheery wave and asked after his Springer Spaniel Teal as she passed.

Jonathan looked more than thrilled to see her. "Oh Tamsin," he said, "the very person!" She waited expectantly. "Teal's .. well, Teal's doing alright really. He's a lovely fellow. But ..."

Tamsin was jostled aside by some tourists squealing with delight as they pointed at the distinctive cider bottles with their black and gold labels.

"You're busy, Jonathan. Drop me an email and we can fix another date - for Teal," she added quickly. She did like Jonathan, and had got on well with him at the time of the contamination scares, but not perhaps as much as he seemed to like her. But he loved his dog, and that was the most important thing for Tamsin. As she walked away, she saw Saffron at the other end of the row of stalls. She was trying to manage her shopping bags, and dropped one on the ground. It spilled some of its contents, and she knelt down and hurriedly scooped them back into the bag, looking around anxiously to see whether she had been noticed. 'Well that's pretty odd,' Tamsin thought to herself, 'what's she hiding?'. She paused to look about to see if anyone else from the class was out taking pictures. And she saw Grace Metcalfe taking a photo of her.

"Hello Grace! Am I part of the Malvern fabric now?" she joked as she walked towards her.

"Oh, I didn't see you there. I was just trying to get that stall there." She looked down at her phone. "But it's all wonky," she sighed. "You're in the class, aren't you?"

"I am. I'm Tamsin. Dogs. You're horses, aren't you?"

"Oh yes. Horses is my main interest. Need to advertise my livery stables, you know." Grace looked flustered and turned to leave. "Cheery-bye!" And she was gone. Tamsin moved further along the Market.

"Boo," she said quietly as she came up behind Emerald, who stood with bulging bags, watching the musicians, where a girl in a long mediaeval-style dress was now dancing with them.

"Ooh, you got here!" Emerald turned, shielding her eyes from the sun. "Got some good pics?"

"Yes thanks. It'll be hard to choose which to submit to Oliver.

They're all *so* good," she chuckled. "You know they're having an exhibition in The Cake Stop at the end of the course?"

"Yes, you said. I'll look forward to seeing that. And talking of The Cake Stop ..."

"Ok. Looks as though your arms are dropping off. Here, give me a bag - I'll need to settle up with you too," she said, as she transferred Quiz's lead to her other hand and took the bag. "Heavens, what did you buy? Bricks?"

"Gary had some lovely potatoes. Couldn't resist, sorry." Emerald's cheeks dimpled as she smiled sweetly. "I got some new season's mushrooms and some beautiful big Hereford onions too."

"Sounds like mushroom soup? It's beginning to get chilly in the evenings."

The two friends set off for their favourite café, chattering about the lovely warming foods they'd be making, now the summer was coming to an end.

"She'll have no more soup either," Tamsin muttered as they reached the café's big glass door.

"Who?"

"Estelle. I'm gripped with all the things she'll never have again. It's so wrong!"

"What's so wrong, dear?" asked a familiar voice, and they looked round to see Quiz happily greeting her friend Muffin, at the end of whose lead stood Charity Cleveland, her grey head tilted inquisitively.

"Charity! Just the person - come and join us." Tamsin held up a hand to forestall any objections. "My treat." And they all entered Jean-Philippe's gorgeously coffee-scented haven.

The café was busy, it being market day, and they had to make do with a table at the back in the more private section of the shop. "Feargal should be dropping by," Emerald confided to Kylie. "Send him over, would you?"

"Of course! But his reporter's nose will surely sniff you out before I can tell him," Kylie twinkled as she spun round to deal with the long queue, her tiny mini-skirt - pink to match her hair - swishing round as she turned.

Once they were all ensconced with their drinks and the inevitable cakes, Charity repeated her question. "What's so wrong, Tamsin?"

Tamsin waved her fork in the air as she finished her mouthful. "Mmm, this new Sticky Toffee Pudding cake is amazing! Must congratulate Damaris on Wednesday."

"Of course. Wednesday, your photography class. How's it going, dear?"

"The class is going great! I'm having terrific fun. But you've heard about the walker Estelle Carruthers?"

"Oh, I did! Saw it in the paper. Quite shocking." Charity tutted, and held Muffin closer to her on her lap.

"Well, Estelle was in that class."

"Was she?" Charity was agog.

"She was. And I've got a sneaky suspicion that the class - or something that happened there, or somebody who's in it - is tied up with her death."

"How do you know?"

"It's the detective's nose," explained Emerald. "She just knows."

"And to be fair, you've never been wrong, my dear. So," she leaned forward eagerly, "tell all!"

Tamsin started to outline what she believed, what she knew, and what she'd actually seen. And it was when she was relating this last, about what she'd seen out and about in town, that Feargal arrived. They cleared a space on the table for his coffee, his toasted sandwich, his large slice of Sticky Toffee cake, and his phone, which he always had ready to hand.

It took no time for him to chomp his way through his toastie, and having assuaged his most urgent hunger pangs, he said, "Well, you may have been right about our mysterious kleptomaniac, Tamsin, old bean."

"Really?"

"There's been no report of thievery since Thursday."

"That's only two days," Emerald pointed out, taking a sip of her lemon tea.

"It was happening on the daily," he went on, pulling his cake towards him and brandishing the fork.

"I just saw Saffron acting a bit suspiciously over the contents of her bag," Tamsin said slowly.

"Saffron? From *Health in the Hills*? Surely not!" Charity clucked.

"Probably nothing. I'm pretty convinced it was Estelle who did all the pilfering. Hey, Feargal, have the police matched the fingerprints on those things we found on Midsummer Hill, now they have her fingers as well?"

Emerald shuddered.

"Haven't heard. But I don't know if she's on their radar."

"If she isn't, then someone ought to put her there," said Charity stoutly.

"I'll have a go," said Feargal, already finishing the last mouthful of his cake.

"Via your underground network?" grinned Emerald.

He gave her a long look and smiled at her. Then turned to Tamsin, reaching out his hand. "Let's have a look at these pictures of yours."

She opened her phone and found the album and handed it to him. "You can zoom in on them - let me show you the people I'm talking about." She leant over the phone and pointed out Estelle, Duncan, and Grace. And then, for fun, showed him Joe Bucket. "And you know Saffron."

He nodded, "Who could forget Saffron - bit of a whirlwind, she is!"

His phone buzzed and he snatched it up from the table. He breathed in sharply. "Well, well, well .." His audience all waited attentively.

"They've taken Janice in for questioning."

CHAPTER THIRTEEN

"No! It can't be Janice! I don't believe it," said Tamsin vehemently. She sat back and folded her arms with a flourish.

"Maybe they're just going for her because she's her sister," Charity suggested.

"You know it's often a family member?" Feargal reminded Tamsin.

"But didn't you say these two were close?" asked Emerald.

"I certainly thought so. And while Estelle was scratchy, Janice seemed very proper and endlessly patient with her. Didn't tell her off or anything, even when she was hurling outrageous accusations about."

"Seems more likely that one of the people she was accusing got shirty about it .." Feargal took a swig of his coffee.

"Well, that was only Oliver, as far as I know. Uh, actually, she complained that Mark's pictures had taken up too much of his attention. And Lucinda's plant photos, now I come to think of it. And horses! That could be me - I had some horse photos. But Grace had *all* horse pictures."

"That's pretty much everyone!" said Emerald. "Mind your feet, Quiz!" she addressed the whirling dervish on the mat beside her chair -

Quiz had had a sudden desire to roll and scratch her back, her legs flailing as she made happy grunting sounds.

Quiz had succeeded in lightening the mood a little. "But," said Tamsin, still smiling fondly at her precious dog, "I can't see that those people would care overmuch - or if they even knew. They may not have heard her."

"Who's to say she didn't complain other times? Maybe directly to them - or at least so that they'd hear." Charity was thinking hard. "People who want to get at other people have lots of sneaky ways to do it, you know."

"True." Tamsin looked glum. "But I'm still convinced she was the thief, and the obvious people to dislike her would be her victims. Do you think they were as random as they appear?"

"You mean she could have been getting her own back on people who'd crossed her in the past?" Emerald's mouth was agape.

"Possible. I've heard madder things," Feargal agreed. "What worried you about Saffron, Tamsin?"

"Oh, just that she was being very furtive about gathering up her things that she spilt out of her bag just now, in the Market." She fidgeted with her teaspoon. "And I'll tell you who else was being furtive," she blurted out, having decided to spill the beans. "Lucinda. You can see her in those photos, Feargal." She took up her phone and found the images again for him. "See there. She's slipping something into her bag and then following Estelle."

"That's another person we should be considering, then," said Charity, re-adjusting Muffin beside her on the chair.

"You don't look very happy about that, Tamsin," Emerald could see her friend's discomfort.

"I'm not. I thought Lucinda was really nice. Honest. Interesting. You know."

"And you don't want to think she's involved?" said Charity.

"I don't."

"But you have to cast your net wide!" Feargal reminded her. "Till you can exclude people."

"She does these amazing drawings of plants and flowers - for authoritative books. I looked some up on the net. They're so detailed, and anatomically correct, of course."

"Do you perhaps mean botanically correct?"

"Oh probably, Mr.Pedant!"

"I think you can have anatomy to do with plants ..." Emerald said dreamily.

"There you go. But for drawings, I expect you're right, Feargal. Anyway, she does lovely work, and is good company and I don't like to think she did anything really bad."

"You work very much on how you feel about people, dear. So you should keep that in mind. But it *would* be nice to know what was going on there."

"Perhaps she followed Estelle by coincidence?" suggested Emerald, always looking for the best in people.

Feargal smiled appreciatively at her. "It's hard to see from these photos. There are gaps. That's a fairly popular passage through to the supermarket. Maybe it was a coincidence."

"And thinking of Saffron for a moment," Tamsin continued. "We already know she has poor judgment when it comes to men. She meets loads of people now she's at the health shop. Oh, and her design business may have caused her to know wotsisname - Duncan?"

"And why did this Duncan geezer arrive at the course a week late? Was he tipped off that Estelle was in it, and thought it a good way to keep an eye on her?" Feargal mooted.

"Most of the students on that course need photography in the pursuit of their business in some way." Tamsin said. "So they're all people who know lots of people - have to, for their living. I knew several people there already, so we can assume that others did too. So I suppose Duncan knowing Grace is not really anything."

"I think we need to find out more about who was robbed," protested Emerald. "How can we find that out, Feargal?"

"I'll see what's new at the station. What they learn from the sister, Janice. I don't know if anything of note ever got reported as stolen."

His phone buzzed again and he peered at the message. "Oh hello! Now this *is* interesting!" He waved the phone about to ensure that they were all listening. "On Estelle's phone they've found an image of her pulling her trolley."

"How could she take a picture of herself?" asked Charity, baffled.

"She didn't take it. It was sent anonymously. That afternoon."

"Can we see the picture?" asked Tamsin breathlessly.

"Just coming through. Here you go," and he turned the phone so she could see the image.

"But that's what she was wearing that day! And look - that's the hat shop she's just passing, on the corner of Graham Road. That must have been taken that day!"

"The day you all had to take photos in town for your assignment," Emerald said quietly, and carried on stroking Quiz's head. "Hey! Where are the shadows? It was a bright day."

"Genius!" Tamsin snatched up her phone and hunted for the pictures she'd taken. Three of them put their heads together and compared them with the one in Feargal's phone.

"You can see the time on my pictures - it's in the metadata."

"In the what?" Charity was floundering.

"The information attached to every photo. So mine were taken at 2.09, 2.11, 2.11, 2.13 ..."

"There's no data with the one on Estelle's phone, of course. But the light looks similar."

"Hey, there's that big old-fashioned clock hanging on one of the buildings in Graham Road. Can you see it?"

"Oh yeah - just. Was a hotel once." Feargal zoomed in. Hard to say. Looks like 1.45."

"I wonder if it's one of those old clocks that tells a different time on each face?" said Charity impishly.

"We'll have to check. One of us can walk down there when we leave here," Tamsin put down her phone. "But on the face of it, it looks as though it was taken around the same time. Actually, that would be before I took the pictures of her. She's coming up the hill - and you know who I snapped further down the hill?"

"Duncan Hattersley and the horse woman," Feargal declared. And they all thought for a moment.

"But who actually sent it to her?" Charity was finding all this tech confusing.

"They don't know, Charity. And it looks as though it's not going to be that easy to find out either. There are all sorts of ways to cover your tracks these days. They *will* trace it," Feargal added with confidence. "But it may take a while."

"So it must be someone who's a bit tech-savvy!" Emerald leant forward in her chair. "That's got to narrow it down a bit."

"It does," Tamsin agreed. "I mean, Damaris wouldn't have a clue - not that anybody would imagine it were her! And Joe Bucket? No idea. But everyone else ... you know all the others could have found out how to do this. Maybe those girls already know, as they live on their phones. Is it easy to find out, Feargal?"

"Afraid so - it's easy enough. A quick search would throw up a few methods - look," he tapped into his search bar and looked at the results. "There are four different methods here, in an instant!"

"I don't like this internet thing," Charity looked very unhappy. "It opens up the way for all sorts of naughtiness."

"I think people have always found a way to be naughty, Charity," Emerald said kindly.

"And on the whole, it's true that it's harder to escape discovery these days than it used to be."

Charity hmph'ed and poured the last of the tea from her teapot. "Why do you suppose someone sent her that picture? Was there a message with it? I mean, a blackmail demand or something?"

Feargal tapped into his phone and waited for it to buzz.

"Yep. Message reads, *We need to talk. Corner Holywell Road at 6. Be there.*"

"Oh no! An invitation to her own murder!" gasped Emerald.

CHAPTER FOURTEEN

"So it's someone with a car!" said Charity triumphantly. Her face fell as the others looked at her. "Well, they could hardly have walked to Midsummer from there, could they?"

"Bit of a trek, yeah."

"That should be easy, then!" said Emerald, brightening up. "The police have cameras everywhere, don't they?"

"Not out here in the sticks!" Feargal laughed. "Very few of them. They have the odd speed camera - but that would only capture an image if the car was speeding at the time."

Emerald frowned. "I wonder .." she said slowly, fondling Quiz's ear and producing an ecstatic expression on the dog's face. "I wonder."

"You wonder?" Feargal said softly.

"What I mean is, if you were going to murder someone, you wouldn't pick them up in your car where anyone could see you. Would you." She looked appealingly at her friends.

"You're right. You wouldn't." Feargal agreed.

"So this message means 'I know what you're doing' and maybe they wanted to meet to blackmail her?"

"By golly, you could be right!" Charity sat on the edge of her seat.

"They wanted to pin her down and tell her to produce some money next time they met."

"No, that won't do," said Tamsin regretfully. "Blackmailers don't expose themselves like that. Secrecy is all important. There must have been some other reason they wanted to meet her."

They all sat silently, thinking hard.

"Someone with a priest complex? Wanted to point out the error of her ways?"

"How about someone who'd had something stolen?"

"And wanted it back!"

"Now there's a possibility!"

"That would suggest they knew she'd taken something of theirs."

"Enough people were robbed. But mostly it was junk she took," Charity pointed out.

"Maybe she was getting bolder?"

"Or maybe she'd pinched the thing she'd been wanting all along, and the rest was to confuse the issue."

Tamsin nodded, "And what she had this time was actually of value!"

"So how would meeting up with her and confronting her help?"

"Force her to return it? Got the evidence on film? Hand it over and I won't take this to the police?"

"So ..." Emerald cut in. "We're looking for someone from the photography class who had had something stolen."

"I bet Duncan and Grace will both show completely different photos on Wednesday. Taken on a different day."

"Pity you didn't take one of him taking photos that day," Emerald said.

"Maybe I did? I'm going to look at these on the computer when we get back. See if I can zoom in further."

"Perhaps you'll be able to see what Lucinda was putting into her bag?"

"Something innocent, I do hope," Tamsin said, feeling deflated.

Charity suddenly sat bolt upright in her chair. "We're all assuming she met that evening with this person who contacted her. But supposing ... she never got there?"

"She'd already been spirited off to Midsummer?" Tamsin perked up. "Ooh, I didn't think of that."

"Now the field has opened right up again," sighed Emerald dejectedly.

"We may have to rely on what the police can find - about cars and cameras," Charity absently twiddled the sleeping Muffin's ear. The dog stretched her paws out dead straight in front of her, then relaxed again.

"What have we got so far?" Tamsin sat up straight and started counting on her fingers. "Estelle died in the car park at the foot of Midsummer Hill on Thursday evening, probably around 7 o'clock. She must have been taken there by someone she knew. Someone has been stealing rubbish from all over town, and it may have been her. We found a bag of swag on Midsummer Hill. Was she going to leave more?" She looked at her hands then switched to counting on the other hand. "Oops, run out of fingers .. Was she going to *collect* some?"

"I'd forgotten the Midsummer significance," Charity nodded. "Of all the Hills, she was killed at the one where stuff had been hidden. It's got to be connected."

"I *suppose*," Tamsin said with great reluctance, "that it could be anyone. Doesn't have to have anything to do with the photography class."

"What about your gut feeling, Mrs.Malvern Hills Detective?" teased Feargal.

"You're right, Feargal! And anyway, the police will have to do the hunting if it's someone we don't know. But I've got this strong feeling, I really have .."

"And you're dying to crack this case. I know you!" laughed Emerald. "Oh hi, Jean-Philippe!" The barista had loomed up behind Tamsin and Feargal.

"I see you are having a council of war, *mes amis?*"

"We are!" Tamsin twisted round to see him.

"And me, I am wondering, '*Pourquoi* did I invite this crowd of trouble-makers to join a class in my upper room?' " As his black eyebrows travelled up his forehead, he smiled benignly. "It is something to do with the class, *n'est-ce pas?*"

"Tamsin thinks it is!" said Emerald. "And hasn't she always been right, up to now?"

"*Up to now*," echoed Tamsin with a crooked smile. "I do hope it's not all going to go wrong. But assuming I'm right, there's two great things about you hosting this class, Jean-Philippe!"

"Two things?"

"Yes! One, I'm on the spot to learn as much as possible about the other students and their possible involvement."

"And the other?"

"And Two, I'm learning to take some great pictures!" She beamed at him, and the mood of the group palpably relaxed.

CHAPTER FIFTEEN

And it was the next morning, after an early walk, that found Tamsin selecting her photos to submit to Oliver for this week's assignment. She had so many! She decided not to include any which had any of the class students in. It would be in bad taste to use the photos of Estelle anyway. And she didn't want to let on that she had spotted anyone that day. But she had plenty to choose from and was able to put the murder out of her mind for a moment and focus on what they had been asked for.

She hummed and hawed over the pictures, and eventually chose two from the supermarket demonstrating the impersonal bustle of the shopping centre, one looking downhill from the Elgar statue reflecting the calmer vibe of the old town centre, and two of the busy Farmers' Market, including a lovely action shot of the girl in her mediaeval outfit dancing in the bright September sunlight. All in all, a definite reflection of the variety her much-loved little town could provide.

Her phone rang with Charity's ringtone - a load of chickens clucking in alarm - and pitched her out of her reverie.

"Hi Charity! How's it going?"

"Hello dear. No, Sapphire, don't sharpen your claws on the sofa.

Muffin, come here please - what have you got? Oh, it's just your teddy bear - that's alright. Now .. where was I?"

"You were saying hello to me, Charity."

"Of course I was! Hello dear, what can I do for you?"

"You rang *me*, Charity."

"Goodness, I'm going batty in my old age. Yes, got it, yes. It was something you said at the tricks class last night, you know, after Cameron had done his lovely 'Bang! You're dead' trick with Buster."

"What did I say?"

"You said, 'It doesn't matter how long it takes to get it, as long as you get it right in the end.' And I thought that maybe we should back-track a bit on this Estelle business."

"Okay?" Tamsin was curious.

"Well, assuming we're right that she was doing the thieving - I think that finding out *why* she was doing it would give us a lead on why she was killed."

"As ever, Charity, you have hit the nail on the head! I was thinking of dropping in on the mourning sister today. See what I can find out."

"Were they very close?"

"Appeared to be. But I don't know if they actually liked each other."

"But she could be shattered, nonetheless. Shall I come with you, dear?"

"I think that would be an excellent idea, Charity, thank you. You can be the angel of the proverb while I'll ever be the fool."

"Rushing in? Maybe, but no-one could ever call you a fool, Tamsin."

So they fixed a time to go down to Malvern Link to the house Janice had shared with her sister Estelle. Before that, Tamsin had time to send off her assignment and get in a good training session with her dogs.

Today she was working on scent. Banjo, her blue merle Border Collie, was doing really well at his Search & Rescue sessions, with the group that served the Malvern Hills. This sort of hunting - often in awful weather - involved a combination of air-scenting and tracking and quartering the ground. The freedom this afforded her occasionally nervous dog was exhilarating for Banjo, and he was always excited when Tamsin put his orange jacket on him to start work.

Dainty long-legged Moonbeam was very good at finding things with her nose - she was more of a general search dog, looking for anything that was out of place, rather than specific human scent. And she was particularly good at getting into tiny spaces to retrieve things that had rolled out of sight, like Banjo's ball under the bookcase! It was her skills that had been instrumental in rescuing Tamsin and Emerald from imprisonment not so long ago ...

And Quiz, a solidly-built dark Border Collie, with one ear down and one enchantingly up, enjoyed the slow, concentrated work of tracking a scent trail. This was normally human scent, but she could equally well apply her skills to the more instinctive pastime of tracking prey. At no time was this clearer than in the snow, or frosty grass, when even our limited human vision could pick out the trails of the beasties - rabbits, hares, deer, birds - and Tamsin loved watching Quiz put her nose down to follow the trail accurately.

Of course, if it was a windy day, she was always amused to notice that Quiz would be following her track a few feet to the leeward side of it, following where the scent was being blown. It was huge what Tamsin had learnt while teaching Quiz - or rather while harnessing her dog's inborn skills and learning to read her dog. She'd explained this to Emerald.

"How can they pick out the smells so clearly?" her friend had asked after watching an early track with Quiz.

"Over a third of the dog's brain is devoted to scent," Tamsin had said, and, encouraged by the sight of Emerald's eyebrows shooting up with surprise, she went on, "They have *hundreds* of hundreds of millions of scent receptors in their noses. Compared with just the very few hundred million we have."

"Wow! I never realised that! Truly they must smell in tech-nicolour!"

And watching her special dog smelling in technicolour was exactly what she was heading out to do now. She'd laid a track earlier - that is to say, she'd walked in a predetermined pattern - for about half a mile, dropping some small objects on the way. She had the use of a neighbour's paddock for this, so she didn't have to worry about cross-tracks from dog-walkers - though there was nothing to stop the rabbits! And now, 2 hours later, she was setting off with Quiz to work the track and recover the objects.

She'd chosen one particularly difficult item today - an old front door key - and she was curious to see if Quiz would manage to find it. Metal doesn't hold that much scent, and hidden in the grass the dog certainly wouldn't see it.

She was not disappointed! Her dog had switched her brain into tracking mode as soon as Tamsin put the leather tracking harness on her and attached the thirty-foot long line, which was how they stayed connected. Nose down, tail up, Quiz cast about busily at the start pole for a full minute before charging off in a straight line. At the first corner she repeated the casting, and locating the right direction, quickly re-attached her nose to the track and pulled forward. She was panting by the time she hurled herself to the ground to indicate that she'd found something. Between her paws was half a wooden clothes peg. Tamsin scooped it up and congratulated her dog, who, having had a quick break, was keen to surge forward again.

And so passed a hardworking half hour. Quiz recovered all three articles, including the metal key, and was only momentarily distracted by a heap of horse dung from the neighbours' ponies. Tamsin took off the harness and tossed Quiz's favourite frisbee for her to chase.

"Hey Quizzy! A great morning's work!" she said, as she wound up the long line, removing some thistle spikes and a couple of burrs from it as she went, "Good girl!" Quiz tossed her frisbee in the air a couple of times then lay down with it, panting. Tracking was hard work!

And feeling thoroughly fulfilled and refreshed, Tamsin returned home to settle her dogs and set out with no little trepidation to meet Charity in the Link.

CHAPTER SIXTEEN

Tamsin met Charity outside Janice's home, and they went to the door together. The door was opened by Janice, her face grey, her eyes red-rimmed.

"Janice, we're so sorry to hear the dreadful news. You know me, Tamsin, from the photography class. This is my friend Charity Cleveland. We wondered if there was anything we could do to help."

Charity stepped forward. "I know how difficult these times can be, my dear. I remember when my mother died - there was just so much to get done, and with all the whirling thoughts in your head, like 'Could I have done more?' and 'I wish I'd told her more often how important she was to me' ..."

"That's just it!" Janice burst out. "There's so much I have to do ... and I miss her so much!" She looked at Charity appealingly, her eyes glistening.

"Let's see what we can do," said Charity, and stepped firmly into the house. As they arrived in the hallway she added, "First thing is to look after yourself. How about a cup of tea? Have you eaten?"

Janice drooped and shook her head dumbly. Charity nodded to Tamsin who headed to the back of the house to find the kitchen and start putting together tea and food. She was soon joined by Charity leading Janice along by the elbow, and the two women sat at the kitchen table, Charity's hands resting gently on Janice's.

It seemed that this silent camaraderie was just what Janice needed, and by the time Tamsin had cups and saucers on the table (this was just the occasion for cups and saucers rather than mugs, she thought to herself) and a cheese sandwich for Janice, she could see that the bereft woman's shoulders had relaxed and she was breathing more evenly.

"Take a bite of the sandwich," Charity ordered. Obediently Janice took a mouthful, realised how very, very, hungry she was and munched her way quickly through it.

"Let me make another," said Tamsin, jumping up from the table and getting to work again.

Janice gave her a strained smile. "Estelle was not the easiest person," she began. "But she was my sister and I did love her really. And you're right Ms Cleveland,"

"Charity, please!"

".. Charity," she nodded. "I wish I'd told her that more often." Before the tears started to flow, Charity pressed her hand again and said, "Tell us about her."

Tamsin marvelled at her friend's ability to soothe this troubled person, and she returned to the table with another plate of food and sat and listened while Janice talked at length about her difficult sister. It seemed that she'd often been passed over at school and at work, which bred a resentment in her which had come out more and more recently.

"She never used to be that critical or tetchy," Janice was saying. "I didn't know what to do. I signed her up for the photography class to encourage her to focus on something new. But she kept finding fault with that too."

After several minutes of this, Tamsin could contain herself no longer. "Did Estelle often go out on walks on her own with her shopping trolley?" she asked, then added very quietly, ".. and not actually do any shopping?"

Janice hung her head. "How did you know?"

"It was just a guess really."

"I think it was - what do they call it? - 'a cry for help'." Janice pressed her lips together to prevent the tears, and Charity held her hand more tightly.

"So .." Tamsin phrased her next question carefully, "do you think that her, um, non-shopping expeditions had anything to do with .. with what happened to her?"

"Oh! I don't know! You see, I have no idea what she was doing up at that car park at Midsummer. When we walked the Hills we'd do it together. I can't imagine ..." Janice's sore eyes gazed out of the kitchen window, which framed the very northern end of the Malvern Hills. "We walked them a lot. I'll have to walk alone now."

Tamsin jumped in to forestall more tears. "Here," she pushed the plate towards Janice, "get stuck into this. It'll do you good."

Janice looked at the sandwich for a moment then started eating it. From her hunger Tamsin wondered whether she'd eaten at all since she'd heard the news.

"Are you saying that .. that .. someone .." Janice was finding it hard to grasp what Tamsin was suggesting. "That it wasn't an accident?"

"It's possible. You see, if Estelle was .. er .. shopping, she may have annoyed someone sufficiently to cause them to challenge her." She paused to let that thought sink in. "So what do you know about what she took?"

"And why do you think she took it at all?" added Charity.

Janice shook her head helplessly. "I really don't know. I don't know why she was doing it. I found out when I came across some of the things people were complaining were missing. I found a supermarket bag with a bicycle chain in, along with a milk carton container for the milkman, and an empty flowerpot. I asked her, of course. She got very flustered and cross and snatched the bag away and went out. I thought maybe she'd give the things back and stop, once she knew I knew. But according to the *Mercury,* she didn't stop. Things kept disappearing."

She took the last of the sandwich and ate it. "And you think someone took the law into their own hands? Surely that's a bit draconian for a few clothes pegs?" she appealed to them.

"I wonder if she'd actually taken something of value - of value to the owner, I mean. Perhaps sentimental value."

"Something they wanted back," added Charity. Janice looked blank.

"So .. was there anyone trying to get in touch with Estelle last week? Anyone asking about her? Tailing her?"

"Anyone showing unusual interest?" Charity put in.

"It's funny. The police asked me loads of questions. But they never said anything about this." Janice passed a hand over her brow and gulped back tears. Charity stood up. "You're exhausted. Here, you need to lie down." She put out a hand to help her up. "Here's my number," she scribbled on an old envelope she pulled from her bag, "Feel free to ring me. Something may come back to you."

Tamsin rose too. "Do let us know if you think of anything. You see, it's wrong. It's all wrong, what happened. And I'd like to help you get justice for your sister."

Janice leant heavily on Charity as she was led to the living room, where Charity settled her on the sofa with and spread a blanket over her.

"Thank you for coming," Janice said weakly, "it was very kind of you." She closed her eyes. "I *will* ring you, Charity, thank you. I'm going to rack my brains and help you find who did this to Estelle." And she leant her head back onto the cushion with a deep sigh and fell instantly asleep.

Charity and Tamsin let themselves out.

CHAPTER SEVENTEEN

"You are amazing!" said Tamsin as they walked back to their cars. "I just don't know how you do it."

"I'm sorry to say it's from years of practice. But you chose the right moments to ask your questions too, dear."

"This confirms that it was definitely Estelle doing the thieving. I looked more closely at those pictures, by the way."

"Anything new?"

"The only new thing was Mark Bendick whizzing down Church Street on his bike."

"Funny that so many of you should have been there at the same time - Estelle, Lucinda, Mark, Duncan, Grace ..."

"Strange indeed. Hey, remember what Feargal was saying about not discounting anyone? And how it's often a family member?"

"I really don't think so in this case. Do you?"

"Nope. You're right. That was genuine. If she wanted to bump off her sister, there would be lots of easier ways, I would think."

"You're so .. down to earth."

"That's one way of describing it!" Tamsin laughed, knowing that the combination of Charity's empathy and her own perspicacity made a terrific team.

They'd reached Charity's car, and with her hand on the door handle, Charity said, "You know who I saw this morning?"

"Who?"

"Saffron. I was in *Health in the Hills* - they do have lovely organic wholemeal flour there."

Tamsin smiled and knew she had to wait and let Charity say things her own way.

"I'm making some scones for Harvest Festival at the church, you see. I do like to do them properly." Charity cast her eyes down modestly, "I'm known for my scones, you know!"

"Deservedly so! And? The health shop?"

"I know Saffron has flights of fancy, but she thinks that your teacher has something to do with it."

"Oliver Barnstaple? No, really. I can't imagine him in the role of murderer."

" 'Don't discount anyone,' weren't we reminded?"

"Ok. I'll leave him in. But most of the class I seem to have eliminated. Damaris, for one. Then I don't see those two girls being bothered by the likes of Estelle - they're far too self-absorbed. Mark, for all his sins, has never been the violent type. Lucinda .." Tamsin sighed. "Well, ok. If Lucinda did it I'd expect her to use a sharpened pencil, or a palette knife or something," she smirked.

"So who does that leave?"

"That leaves," Tamsin screwed up her eyes as she thought, "Niamh O'Connor, the teacher; Saffron; Joe the gardener; Duncan Hattersley; and Grace Metcalfe."

"And Oliver?"

"And Oliver."

"You know what, Charity?" Tamsin said with sudden resolve. "I think we need to talk to Niamh. And Grace. Want to come?"

"Try keeping me away! But I think Emerald may be a good person to have with you to talk to Niamh. She's young, isn't she?"

"Youngish, yes. Good idea. Emerald has class at The Cake Stop tonight though. Perhaps we could go round straight after. It won't be too late. I believe Niamh lives in Hanley Swan."

Charity raised a querying eyebrow.

"I sneaked a look at the register." Tamsin grinned.

"There's no flies on *you*, young Ms Kernick!"

"Handy, isn't it? So Niamh's in Hanley Swan - I'll have a go at her tonight. Grace now - she's got her horse place out Leigh Sinton way. Shall we go?"

"No time like the present!"

"Here, I'll drive. My van's just up here."

Grace's stables had a look of faded grandeur. The hanging sign over the five bar gate had long since faded and started to peel. The gate had dropped with age and needed a lift and a mighty heave to open it. They drove up the weedy drive towards the house at the end. Either side of them were paddocks with some very healthy-looking horses in.

"At least the animals are well cared for," Tamsin said approvingly as they slowed down to park the van next to an old Volvo Estate and a double horse box with *Metcalfe's Livery* written across the back. There was no answer from the house, so they walked into the stable yard which, surprisingly, was very attractive. Here the loose boxes were treated timber, the paths were concrete and washed clean, and there were even some tubs of flowers in the centre of the grassed yard, which was mown neatly.

"It's clear where her values lie!" Charity said quietly, as they heard raised voices from one of the boxes up the yard, identifiable by the wheelbarrow parked outside with a dung fork standing up in the straw.

"I've told you this isn't good enough!"

"I'm sorry Miss Metcalfe, I thought I done it right," came the muted reply.

"These animals are valuable. Their bedding must be kept perfectly clean."

"I'm sorry Miss Metcalfe."

"We can't have stained horses - if you want to stay here you'd better look lively!"

"I do, Miss Metcalfe. I will. I love horses!"

"Then do this box again. You girls are useless! I'll come and check it in half an hour."

"Yes Miss Metcalfe. I'm sorry Miss Metcalfe."

There was a bang as the loose box door was slammed behind the emerging Miss Metcalfe. She looked up in surprise at her visitors, realised she must have been overheard and adopted a smile as she strode towards them. "Training up a new stable girl," she honked. "We only have the best here."

She clearly thought her visitors were possible customers, so Tamsin was quick to disabuse her.

"I'm sure you do! I'm Tamsin, from the photography class, and this is my friend Charity. She just *loves* horses and of course I love dogs," she chattered on breathlessly, "and we were passing and realised this must be your place. And we thought - didn't we Charity?" Charity nodded vigorously. "We thought that maybe we could drop in and have a look. The horses we could see from the road look marvellous. You don't mind, do you? It's Grace, isn't it?"

Grace stood in two minds. She really didn't want to bother with them, but just maybe the old lady could lead to a customer. "Certainly," she said after a pause. "What do you want to see?" Without waiting for an answer she turned on her booted heel and started walking purposefully along the boxes. Horses' heads were peering over the doors.

"Do they think it's feed time?" asked Tamsin.

"They're curious, that's all." Grace was rather short with her. Perhaps people skills don't rate very highly with her, thought Tamsin. It was sadly so often the way with those who chose to devote their lives to animals - because of their inability to get on with people. And she thought of all the dog trainers she'd come across who were - as the polite saying goes - 'challenged' in dealing with their fellow humans.

So she asked lots of questions as they walked along. "What's this one called?"

"That's Nelson."

"Oh, he's so big! And this little white horse next door to him?"

"The grey?" Grace looked down her nose at Tamsin - difficult because she was several inches shorter. "Her name's Stella."

"Stella!" Charity gasped. "Wasn't that the name of the woman who died in suspicious circumstances last week?" Her eyes were round.

"That was Estelle, I believe. And I didn't know her death was suspicious? What makes you say that?"

Charity leaned in, glancing round her before she spoke in a whisper, "They say she was hit on the head." She shut her mouth firmly, stood up straight again, and folded her arms.

"But you knew her, Grace - she was in our class," exclaimed Tamsin. "How do you think she died?"

"I really wouldn't know." Grace walked on. "This is the tack room," and indicated a room with the sweet smell of leather wafting through the door.

Tamsin peered in, "You won all those rosettes!" she thought a little more focus on Grace would help. "What are they for?"

"Mostly eventing," grunted Grace. "Some dressage as well." Tamsin coo-ed in admiration.

Charity had stepped into the room and was looking at the grooming tools laid out on a table. "I bet these are expensive," she said. "Did you get any pinched by that madman who's going round stealing things?"

"I did not. This yard is busy all day and locked at night, with a chain on the entrance gate." Then she turned and peered at Charity. "What makes you say it's a 'madman'. Have they caught someone?"

"Oh no, they haven't. At least, as far as I know they haven't. I only know what I read in the *Malvern Mercury*," she simpered.

"That rag!" snorted Grace, who had turned and started back along the path, having decided she'd had enough of this pair, and that they were after all unlikely to furnish her with a horse for livery.

"Oh, don't you like it? I find it very entertaining. Don't they do write-ups of your events? You must have been mentioned in despatches, with all these prizes you've won?" Charity smiled broadly in appeasement, as she trotted to keep up with the striding horsewoman.

"Last time they sent some red-headed idiot who didn't know a hoof from a tail. Spelt my name wrong," she huffed, and Tamsin coughed loudly into her hanky to prevent herself bursting into giggles.

"So sorry!" she said as she mopped her nose. "Thank you so much for showing us round." Grace looked at her with disdain. Tamsin turned and looked at the looming shape of the North Hill. "Do you ride on the Hills?" she asked, as if as an afterthought.

"In places. Much of the Hills is too steep for horses."

"There's a gentle path up to Midsummer, is there not?"

"There is. You can access it from the Eastnor side."

"Ah, right. I know the car park side is very steep. We've puffed our way up that hill, haven't we, Charity."

"We certainly have. It must be wonderful to ride along the top of the Malverns! Those views! All that fresh air! You know, when I was a girl ..."

But Grace had no interest in Charity's girlhood memories, and interrupted to say, "Make sure you shut the gate on your way out," and turned on her heel, roaring, "Mandy? Have you done that box yet?" as she stomped back up the yard.

Tamsin watched her arrive at the loose box with the barrow outside, and looking at the barrow she suddenly froze and hissed, "The trolley! Where's her trolley?" and jumping into the van, hurriedly texted Feargal with that very question.

CHAPTER EIGHTEEN

Tamsin found Emerald at Pippin Lane when she got back and brought her up to speed.

"And so you've been volunteered to come with me to talk to Niamh this evening."

"But I have class .."

"I know. *After* your class, ninny!" she smiled as she glanced at her friend to make sure her jibe was taken as it was meant.

"Ok, that would be fun! What's she like?"

"Teacher at Cameron's school. Somewhere between your age and mine. Nearer yours, I think. And she seems to be of the *genus* Mouse."

"Goodness! How does she manage a class of 10-year-olds if she's a mouse?"

"I think you're right .. I think she's probably not as mouselike as she would like to appear. We'll see! I can pick you up from The Cake Stop a bit after 8 - ok?"

"Ok!" Emerald gave Opal a parting snuggle, picked up her yoga bags and set off, floating gracefully out of the back door.

Tamsin settled down with a coffee, Moonbeam on her lap, to do some class planning for her next Dog Tricks Class. She had to be sure to give the students tricks which were accessible both to the dog and the owner. Some dogs just aren't made for rapid movement or acrobatics - nor are some owners! So she was working out a varied program where everyone would be able to find tricks they could enjoy without fear of injury. The most explosive and noisy trick would definitely be the one that Cameron and his little brothers would choose for Buster!

She took a break to take the dogs in the garden and enjoy the last of the cool evening. She looked up at the towering Malverns, now blue and grey in the shade. The sun had long disappeared behind the Hills, though it would be daylight for another hour or so. The rose bush that always grew long arcs of branches was still covered with pale pink blooms, with some Michaelmas daisies peeping their mauve heads through the rosy tangle. She grabbed a toy from the grass and, setting Banjo up beside her, she said "GO!" and as he shot forward she threw the toy over his head for him to chase to the end of the garden and snatch up.

She loved the trembling anticipation in the dog as he knew what was coming and stared intently forward, then the burst of energy as he leapt up and raced ahead, confident that the toy would arrive.

She did a few throws for Quiz as well, and asked Moonbeam to hop up onto the picnic table for some pirouettes and twists and twirls.

And having fed the dogs and herself - of course! - she set off to town to collect Emerald. Opal had an all-day buffet which hadn't currently needed topping up.

At this time of night she was able to pull up right outside the café, and was happy to stand and chat with the yoga students as they emerged. They all had a warm glow and a serenity about them. Perhaps I should try this calming stuff, she thought, as she greeted Linda, one-time ballerina and owner of the health shop, who was talking to Shirley - the mother of Mark the cyclist and owner of the tremendous Pyrenean Mountain Dog Luke - as they came out through the big glass front door.

"What brings you here, Tamsin?" asked the petite Linda with a broad smile.

"Just going to spirit your teacher off somewhere. How did it go?"

"Lovely, as usual," she replied.

"If only all the world would practice yoga," said Shirley dreamily, "it would be a far better place."

"Did you know there's a Government Minister for Yoga in India?" Tamsin surprised her by asking.

"I didn't!" squeaked Shirley with astonishment. "Maybe that's why they're so peaceable as a nation?"

"They have a Yoga day when everyone does yoga in the street. This year the theme is the empowerment of women. Emerald was telling me all about it."

"That's amazing - we certainly need empowering!" Molly had joined them, with Cameron standing quietly beside her.

"How did you do this evening, Cameron," Tamsin asked the young boy.

"It was brilliant! I can do a wheel better than anyone else - except Emerald, of course. She's absolutely wizard."

"It's not a competition, darling," admonished Molly. "We all do our best and it's what works for each of us."

"Yes, Mum, I know," he said with resignation. "But I *was* jolly good at it, wasn't I?"

They all laughed at the charming youngster, and Tamsin said quietly to him, "Perhaps you could use a wheel for your next trick with Buster?"

"Yeah! He could jump over me!"

"And stand on your tummy - or roll under you, or weave round your arms and legs .. lots of possibilities. Have a think about it."

Cameron started to jump up and down enthusiastically, just like his brother Alex. "I can't wait to get home .."

"It's a school day, so not tonight, Poppet. Tomorrow after homework will do fine."

The little boy exaggeratedly folded his arms with a flourish and put on a grumpy face, but couldn't hold it for long. He was chattering animatedly to his mother as they went to find their car.

"What do you think about this latest murder, Tamsin?" whispered Shirley. "And don't tell me you're not involved, because I just *know* you must be!"

"It's true I did meet the victim. As did Mark."

"Did he? He never told me?"

"Not interesting enough for him, perhaps. She was at our photography class."

"Oh! I didn't know."

"And the teacher dun it!" Saffron had arrived noisily with the group on the pavement. Her black curls were sticking to her brow as a result of her exertions in the yoga class. Her yoga bag fell open, spilling some of its contents. Tamsin put a foot out to stop the water bottle rolling away.

"Oh, thank you, Tamsin. Goodness ..."

"Why do you think the teacher did it?" she asked as she handed her the bottle.

"He's so weird! Looks just like an owl. 'And today's assignment,' " she mimicked in a snooty voice.

"I don't think that's a capital crime, Saffron, looking like an owl. I can think of a lot worse things to look like," smiled her boss, Linda.

"No, but I'm sure Tamsin already knows *lots* of incriminating things about him!" she giggled.

"You want to be careful saying things like that out loud, Saffron. Walls have ears, you know!" Tamsin added quietly. "For all we know, that's why Estelle was killed."

"Oops! Ok. I'll just tell *you*."

"Seriously, anything you can think of that may help, I'd like to know."

"You *are* investigating! How terribly exciting! There's no peace for the wicked with you around," and she bounced away, catching her flapping cardigan on a litter bin. Stopping to unhitch herself rather spoiled her exit.

"How's she doing at *Health in the Hills*?" Tamsin asked Linda.

"Let's just say that, between her and Rosie, there's never a dull moment!"

"That's good to hear. I'm glad it's worked out so well. What's up, Shirley?" Tamsin had noticed that Shirley had gone quiet and was chewing her lip.

"Oh .. nothing."

"Mark's doing so well now. You're not worried about him, are you?"

"I think mothers always worry," Linda looked kindly at Shirley.

"I'm fine, thanks," and Shirley gave herself a shake, as Emerald finally came through the big door and locked it.

"There you are!" Tamsin called out in a cheery voice. "All done?"

"Yep, thanks. Had to be sure I wasn't locking anyone in."

"You need one of my search dogs to sweep the place when you leave!"

"Great idea. I wondered what was so odd about you - you have no dog with you."

"Night all!" Tamsin waved as she clicked her key to open the van, and held open the back door for Emerald to stow her yoga class gear.

"Off on the detective trail," she grinned at her friend as both got in and slammed the doors. "Let's go!"

CHAPTER NINETEEN

It didn't take them long to get to the village of Hanley Swan and locate Niamh O'Connor's house. It was a quite large, old, four-square, Georgian house. "Bit grand for a primary school teacher? I guess she must have a room," Tamsin pulled on the hand-brake.

"Feels odd, just turning up," said the sensitive Emerald.

"Yeah, but you know it works."

"Is true. We've done it enough times now," she smiled back as they got out of the van and crunched their way up the gravel path to the front door. Sure enough, there they found three bells, and pressed the one with the stuck-on scrap of paper with Niamh's name on.

They could hear footsteps drumming down the staircase, and saw the slender shape of the girl as she stood behind the stained glass of the front door to unbolt it. She looked at them with a fresh but puzzled face.

"Oh, it's Tamsin, isn't it?" she smiled as recognition dawned.

"That's right! And this is my chum Emerald. We were passing and noticed that we were near your house, so .. we thought we'd drop in."

Niamh's mouth opened as if to object. "You see, Emerald would love to see some of your playground pictures," Tamsin added quickly.

Niamh blushed. "Sure and what would you be wanting to look at my photos for? They really aren't very good."

"Emerald does yoga, you see, so she's really interested in capturing movement - and you did that so well in your photos last week."

Niamh gave herself a shake, "But of course you can see them - do come in." And she turned and ran up the stairs ahead of them.

"What a charming room!" said Emerald as they entered her door at the top of the stairs. It was a light room, with big windows. There was a majestic marble fireplace, with lots of postcards wedged on top of it, just below a framed landscape of dark hills running down to crashing seas. In the corner was a single bed, covered with a quilt and big cushions to make it into a day-bed, and above it a big holy picture of the Sacred Heart. Along with two armchairs there was a wooden table and a couple of upright dining chairs to complete the room.

"Yes, it is lovely, isn't it? I've got a couple of rooms here. I was lucky to find this place."

Tamsin gazed out of the tall three-sash bay window, admiring the garden below, leaving Emerald to do the ice-breaking.

"I know, it can be so hard, can't it - finding the right place. I struck lucky too. I had to find somewhere I could bring my cat!" Emerald pointed to a stack of exercise books on the table. "Marking?"

"Yes," sighed Niamh. "It seems never-ending. But I do enjoy teaching!"

"What school are you at?"

"Lower Thatchall Junior School. It's a small little village school - just staying open by the skin of its teeth."

Tamsin's ears pricked up and she walked over from the window. "It's going to close?"

"It *was* going to close, then this family moved to the village with three boys - and they have a little girl too - and it just moved the numbers up enough to save the school."

"That would be Cameron, Alex, and Joe?" asked Emerald.

"Yes!" Niamh gazed at her in surprise. "Do you know them?"

"We do indeed," replied Tamsin with a laugh. "I first met them when they brought their terrier puppy to one of my dog training classes."

"Of course! That's what you do, isn't it, dog training." She nodded vigorously. "I'm looking forward to seeing your assignment when you show us your pictures of dogs! We always had a dog at home," she said wistfully, glancing up at the picture over the mantelpiece.

"Let's see *your* photos, Niamh," Emerald reminded her, and they all sat down on the sofa to admire Niamh's pictures.

After suitable compliments, and much mirth when Tamsin spotted Joe chasing a couple of girls across the playground, Tamsin asked how she was doing with the town assignment.

"I enjoyed it! I was up there the very next day, after school. I had an idea of where I wanted to take pictures and couldn't wait till the weekend."

"Thursday? And what spot did you choose?"

"Just opposite the Library. I wanted to catch just a few people going in and out there rather than the town centre where they're busy doing their messages."

"That's Graham Road, isn't it?" Tamsin glanced meaningfully at Emerald. "Do let us see!"

And Niamh scrolled on to find a big batch of photos she'd taken.

"I haven't gone over them yet," she chattered, "I was planning to pick the ones for my assignment tonight and send them over." She frowned, "Oh, some of these are a bit blurry .."

"They're fine," Tamsin encouraged her, "I like this one." And she pointed to a picture of the Malvern townsfolk going about their business. In the photo she spotted a figure weaving through the crowds pulling a shopping trolley behind her.

"Yes. Lots of people!" Niamh grinned with pleasure, apparently quite unaware of the figure progressing along the pavement. They flipped to the next picture. Here Tamsin and Emerald could clearly see Estelle and her trolley going into the Library. Scrolling through several more photos, there was no sign of her emerging. But there *was* something that caught Tamsin's eye.

"Look!" said Tamsin, "I do believe that's Joe Bucket in that rickety old jeep."

"With the trailer?" asked Emerald.

"Yes, that one. He's just going past the Library .." But that was the last they saw in the photos of any of their classmates. Tamsin handed the phone back to its owner and abruptly changed the subject.

"What do you think of this murder, then?"

"The woman on the Hills? Awful! Wonder who she was .."

"But you knew her!"

"I did? B-but .." Niamh started to stammer. "I saw it in the paper. I didn't notice the name."

"She was sitting in front of you last Wednesday. In the front row."

"Those two sisters? Oh my gosh! I had no idea. Really?" She frowned then looked up with her big round blue eyes, "You must think I'm awful! So callous .. But I had no idea! Why would anyone want to kill her? She seemed pretty innocuous to me."

Tamsin made a mental note. Niamh seemed to know which sister it was, otherwise her first question would have been 'Which one?'.

"Hard to say. I wondered if you might have any ideas - you're such a sensitive sort of person. But .. maybe you don't."

"Oh - I don't know. I saw them at the class alright. But didn't even remember their names. I *do* remember the shorter one ..."

"That would be Estelle."

".. Estelle. I do remember her being quite argumentative with Oliver. And her sister. Bit prickly altogether." She turned her goggling eyes to Tamsin, "And she was *murdered?*"

"It looks like it. Have you seen her since the class? Thursday, I mean."

"No. No. Not at all."

"Let me look at those photos of yours again."

Niamh opened her phone with a puzzled expression and located the pictures.

"There you go. That's her." Tamsin pointed out the woman with the trolley.

Niamh gasped. "That must have been .. not long before she died. How horrid, I must delete them!" But before she could tap the delete button, Tamsin put out her hand to stop her.

"They may be important evidence."

"But I don't want them in my phone!" wailed Niamh.

"Tell you what. Send them to me. Then you can delete them. If they're needed some time, they can get them from me. That'll get them out of your phone safely! All the metadata will come with them." She saw a cloud of bafflement descend over Niamh's face. "All the information about when and where it was taken," she clarified. And so did Niamh's face.

"Thank you! I had no idea .." Niamh muttered, "no idea at all. Now, how do I send them to you?"

A quick lesson later and the photos were safely stowed in Tamsin's phone. She emailed them to herself straight away to be sure to be sure, as the very slightly Irish Feargal might say, but the totally Irish Niamh had not yet uttered. "Now you can delete them."

"I've just realised - if you hadn't pointed it out, I could have submitted those photos for my assignment. That would have been dreadful when they're all shown blown up on the screen!"

"Really glad we dropped by," said Emerald soothingly, as they rose to leave. "Have fun with your pupils - especially those three boys!"

"Aw, they're such pets, so they are!" said a greatly-relieved Niamh.

"They are, aren't they. A lovely family," agreed Tamsin as they said their goodbyes to leave Niamh's home in Hanley Swan.

"Do you think she's really as clueless as she makes out?" asked Emerald as they crunched back down the drive.

"Good catch! I don't think so at all. All that flimflam about not knowing who Estelle was - she clearly knew exactly."

"Why do you think she wanted to pretend she didn't?"

"That's the question. Why did she lie? At the moment I have no idea."

It was only when they got back to the *Top Dogs* van that Tamsin checked her messages.

"They've taken Mark Bendick in for questioning!"

"No!" the two women chorused together.

With a grim expression, Tamsin whammed the van into gear and they set off for home.

CHAPTER TWENTY

Next morning, Tamsin plodded drowsily - and her dogs thundered delightedly - down the stairs to find Emerald already making the coffee.

The dogs flew out to the garden, Moonbeam giving a couple of yaps to tell a pigeon to clear off. Tamsin picked up their water bucket and took it to the sink to wash and refill. And while there she took the opportunity to lean over and inhale the intoxicating scent coming from the cafetière. The ever-hungry Opal was miaowing plaintively, smarming herself round Emerald's ankles, and was shortly rewarded by food being dolloped into her bowl. She jumped up softly and, settling onto her haunches, got to work on the food, purring loudly.

"I wonder what news there is this morning about Mark," Emerald poured two coffees.

"Awful. They must be quite wrong. Perhaps we should drop round to see Shirley? She'll be having kittens, worrying about her errant son!" Tamsin replaced the water bucket by the garden window, opening the door to let the dogs in again. "You free this morning?"

"Got a private later on. Let's find out the news first."

"Good thought, Boy Wonder."

"Why is it that bad things always seem to be happening to our friends, and people we know?" Emerald asked sadly.

"It's because we live in an enchanting small town and we've woven our lives into its rich pattern."

"Wow - you're poetic this morning!"

"We're getting to be like Charity - knowing everyone."

"We could never be like Charity! She's a living historical encyclopaedia."

"True. She *is* amazing, isn't she?" Tamsin accepted her steaming mug and held it under her nose. "I wonder what she'd have to say about Mark?"

"Let's ask her."

"You're ahead of me - bit early for my brain to be functioning. Yes! I'll ring her now." Tamsin spirited up Charity on her phone, amused as ever at the image of her friend frowning into the camera struggling to take a selfie, and turned on the speaker for Emerald's benefit.

"Wotcher Charity!"

"Oh, oh, Tamsin! Good morning, my dear."

"Have you heard the latest?"

"About Estelle?"

"Mark Bendick's been taken in for questioning."

"Well, that, if I may say so, is ridiculous! What *can* Inspector Hawkins be thinking?"

"There you go, Emerald. Charity agrees with us. Same knee-jerk reaction."

They seemed to have lost Charity for a moment as they heard her muffled voice, "Sapphire, please take the mouse outside again. You know we don't have mice in the house .." Charity came through loud and clear again, "Of course, dear. For all his faults, Mark is a kind boy. Foolish, but kind. He's never done anything like that."

"We're going to see if Shirley's ok. Hope they'll be letting him out soon."

"I jolly well hope so too!" said Charity as they ended the call.

"Strong words from Charity! Let's have breakfast and go over to Shirley Vaughan's."

When they arrived at Shirley's, driving through the gate between the enormously tall dark hedges and up to the front of her hacienda-style house - so inappropriate in the Severn Valley - they saw Luke, the big white Pyrenean Mountain Dog, lying on the verandah in the shade from the autumn sunshine. He looked up, ready to raise the alarm at the intruders, recognised Tamsin getting out of the van and instead lay back down, his mighty tail thumping on the wooden decking.

"Hi Luke, where's your Mum?" But before she could reach the bell, a flustered Shirley emerged from the front door.

"Oh, it's you. Hallo. I thought you may be ..." a tear fell from her puffy eyes. She'd clearly been crying. "Something awful's happened."

"We heard."

"That's why we came round, Shirley," said Emerald.

"No news from the station?" asked Tamsin. "They've got it wrong, you know."

"Of course they have. Just because Mark has a record they try and pin everything on him! Don't they remember how helpful he was over that bike shop business?" She waved her arms helplessly. "Can't they ever let his past go?" Shirley started to weep properly, which got Luke to his feet. He came over and pressed his big head against her hip. She held his head and leaned over to kiss him. Tamsin led her to the table and they sat on the metal chairs. Tamsin had forgotten how remarkably uncomfortable these chairs were, and after a cool night she could feel the cold from the metal seat penetrating her trousers.

"I'm sure he'll be back soon," soothed Emerald.

Now Shirley was seated, Luke pressed his head against her shoulder.

"He's a great support dog, Shirley."

Shirley mopped her eyes and gave Luke another hug. "He is. I don't know what I'd do without him." She smiled at her dog, her face crumpled. "It's just because he was in town that day, that's all. But that doesn't mean he *did* anything. Anyway, how could he have taken Estelle to Midsummer? He only has a bike."

"Does he not have his motorbike any more?"

"Oh, yes, he has that still."

"So he could take a passenger on it?"

"I never thought of that!" Shirley gasped.

"You may be sure the police have. Where is the bike?"

"It's round the back under cover."

"I imagine you'll either be seeing Mark soon when they let him out, or they'll be round to look over the bike for evidence."

"Oh Lord ... He's a good boy, really he is!"

How many times had Tamsin heard Shirley saying that? How she had suffered with all his goings-on down the years, Mark always in danger of being sucked in from the borderline of crime into the deep well from which few escaped. But she had to agree.

"I don't think he'd hurt anyone on purpose."

"Has anyone told *Flying Pedals* why he's not in?" asked Emerald.

Shirley looked stricken.

"Here, I'll do it. I'll talk to Sara if I can. She'll smooth things over." And Emerald walked away to ring the bike shop where Mark was the chief mechanic. "Trying to get signal .." she muttered as she went out of sight round the side of the house, holding her phone up in the air to trap the errant radio waves.

Tamsin thought for a moment, then asked Shirley, "How do you know he was in town that day?"

"Well, he's in town every day, isn't he, at the shop. And he told me he was taking pictures round town for his photography homework the day they found that woman."

"He may have something interesting in the pictures he took! When he arrives home, tell him I'd like to have a look." Tamsin stood up. "In fact, I'll tell him myself! I have every confidence he'll be at the photography class this evening." She looked down at the desperate mother. "They're pretty good, our police, you know," she added quietly.

Shirley snorted, "Hmph."

Emerald came back round the house. "Done!" she said, waving her phone. "Sara will sort everything."

"Look after your mother, Luke," said Tamsin, offering her hand for the big dog to sniff.

They took their leave of Shirley and Luke and set off up the drive again, pausing between the ends of the giant dark green hedge.

"Take a look at the bike?" asked Tamsin, as she checked the road was clear before pulling out.

"Uh-huh. It's there alright. With one helmet. I didn't touch it, but the tyres are quite dirty. As if he's been off-road on it."

"I wonder ..." said Tamsin, as they headed home.

CHAPTER TWENTY-ONE

By the time she got home, having dropped Emerald off on the way for a private session at the home of one of her clients, Tamsin found a stack of messages on her phone.

There was one from Feargal, which simply said:

No news re Mark. Will keep you posted. Haven't heard anything about trolley.

Surprisingly there was one from Niamh, saying:

Not sure I'll be there tonight. Awful headache. Please tell Oliver.

"Of course, she had my number from sending me the pictures yesterday. Not as tech-averse as she suggested. Puzzling," was all she said, as she flipped to the next message. The nearest dog tilted her head to try to interpret this rambling, with no success.

"Aha!" The next message was from Maggie, and she instantly rang her. And fortunately Maggie was in a position - in her office at the police station rather than up to her elbows in the mortuary - to answer.

"Hi Maggie! Thanks for your text - what news from the PM?"

"Death caused by fractured skull," said the forthright pathologist quietly. "Nothing exciting, I'm afraid. Here," she said in a louder voice, "time we enjoyed a dog walk together. Jez would love to see Quiz again!"

Tamsin realised that Maggie was guarding her words because of where she was. "That would be lovely! It's such a beautiful day today, and I'm free this afternoon - how about it?"

"I'll be home after lunch so I can pick up Jez - three-ish? I thought instead of Herefordshire, for a change we might check out somewhere nearer to you this time. Seeing as we're now approaching Autumn?"

Tamsin grinned. "See you at three!" And she ended the call wondering what news she'd hear from Maggie on Midsummer Hill.

She did have a living to earn, though, and turned her mind to her next two home visits. The first, at Earl's Croome, was to an old lady whose even older dog was nearly as deaf as she was, and both needed some help in dealing with this new situation. The other, straight after, in Twyning, was the sort of home visit Tamsin loved - an eleven-week-old puppy with a first-time dog owner. Such a pleasure to be able to show the owner the best way to interact with their new companion, with no shouting and no No's! And the owners were always amazed and delighted at how clever their little puppy appeared to be, and how quickly the pup could grasp what they had previously considered advanced concepts.

She stocked her training bag with a variety of treats and training gear. As she'd already sourced the best tools for the job - in terms of leads, harnesses, toys, and the like - she was able to sell these direct and make a few extra shillings on the visit. And it would be very surprising if the new puppy-owner didn't sign up for the next puppy course.

So she was feeling satisfied and expansive by the time she reached the car park at Midsummer a bit before three. She was leaning against the van, tossing the frisbee up the hill for Banjo and Moonbeam while Quiz sniffed the grass and the last of the summer's flowers, when Maggie's big black car rolled into the car park, its tyres crunching noisily on the sun-baked stony ground.

Maggie helped Jez out of the back of the car, and once free the old dog made a bee-line for his friend Quiz. They carried on their companionable mooching and sniffing together. They were studying the big boulders that marked the edge of the car park, when they stiffened and fixated on the edge of one of them.

"There's your answer," said Maggie, after giving Tamsin a friendly hug.

"That's where she died?"

"It is. I saw all the photos, of course."

"That was a week ago and the dogs can clearly pick it up still. I never cease to marvel at their scenting ability. It's a closed book to us."

"Didn't you tell me once that dogs on a boat can scent a body on the bed of a deep lake?"

"I did. They can! But I always find it enthralling when I actually see it happening."

"What they can't tell you, is *how* it happened. I didn't want to mention it on the phone, but there are clear signs that there was some kind of tussle."

Tamsin turned to face Maggie fully, raising her eyebrows expectantly.

"Her upper arms had been gripped. She was a wiry old bird, but the marks are clear. She had a bruised shoulder - that would be commensurate with the fall onto the boulder. And one of her wrists had torn skin. There's also a faint indication of bruising on the chest, where she may have been shoved."

"Any chance the wound was inflicted by a horse?"

"Nope."

"Hmm. Just a thought. It was definitely the boulder that did for her?"

"Definitely. Matches the head injury perfectly from the photos I've seen. Right at the base of the skull. Let's have a look." They wandered over to the boulder. Quiz and Jez had by now lost interest and were over on the grass at the foot of the hill, along with Banjo and Moonbeam. Moonbeam gave Jez a sniff and a brisk wag of her flagpole-like tail, while Banjo chose to keep his distance, his mouth clamped onto his frisbee.

The boulder was rough-hewn, and there were a number of places where contact with the back of the head would not have been good news. But seeing the point the dogs had indicated, Maggie nodded her head slowly. "Yep, that would do it alright."

"So we can assume that whoever was here with her that day argued with her. I imagine the marks on the chest suggest she was pushing towards them and they pushed back. But gripping the upper arms?"

"That would be typical if you were trying to stop someone hitting you. Also the twisted skin on one wrist. Was this Estelle a fighter?"

"I'd guess, yes. From what little I knew of her, she seemed pretty feisty." Tamsin thought for a moment as she looked at the rock. "She was arguing with the person who'd brought her here. It got physical ... Impossible to know, I should think, whether her death was intentional or not?"

"From the physical evidence we have, not possible. I think Hawkins will be relying on a confession to turn this from manslaughter to murder."

"But definitely not accident. Let's walk," said Tamsin, giving her dogs a shout. "I feel the need of some fresh air."

"Plenty of it up there," smiled Maggie, nodding to the top of the escarpment. "I may need to tack up the hill, to make it easier for Jez."

"Sure. Let's start over there."

And so they ascended Midsummer Hill in a leisurely manner, and relaxed into the beauty of the wild hill, the trees and ground cover on the way up, and the dramatic views from its summit, not to mention some early blackberries from the clumps growing beyond the stunted trees at the top below the earthworks, which all six of them enjoyed eating. The dogs picked the lower ones while Maggie and Tamsin chose the lushest from the higher branches.

It was on the way down that it happened.

The dogs had all fanned out, as ever following their noses. And Quiz followed her nose under a clump of bracken. She spun round and lay down, looking expectantly at Tamsin.

"Whatcher got, Quizzy?" She recognised her dog's signal that she'd found something, and trotted over to peer into the undergrowth. Her manner changed abruptly.

"Maggie! Over here!" She held up the fronds of bracken to reveal - a shopping trolley!

"I recognise it. It's Estelle's. I've been wondering where it was, because we know she had it in town that day.

"Well, well - we'll have to get you on the force, Quiz!" Quiz, who'd got her reward and been released, had already rejoined Jez and was now happily sniffing the ground with him. "You're sure it's hers?"

"Quite sure - that faded beige check pattern. I wonder if there's anything in it." She reached forward.

"Hold hard!" said Maggie, putting out a hand. "We can't touch it. I'll ask the guys whether they want me to bring it in, as I'm here."

A brief phone call later, and she said, "I'm to take some photos of it *in situ* and bring it back. Step back for a moment so I don't include you in the photos too!" Maggie grinned.

"Ha! That would never do!" Tamsin rejoined the dogs over nearer the quarry.

After taking a few shots from different angles, Maggie said, "Stay there while I get a picture from further away, and get my gloves from the car."

And she returned wearing her blue nitrile gloves, picked up the trolley by its side and carried it down to her car, laying it on the back seat. She carefully lifted the bag slightly open and peered inside with the aid of her torch.

"Looks like some string."

"And isn't that a plastic flowerpot?" asked Tamsin, peering too.

".. and a rather old and muddy garden trowel. Her last bits of thievery."

They stood in silence for a moment, till Tamsin said, "She still didn't deserve to be killed."

CHAPTER TWENTY-TWO

Tamsin chose to skip any coffee chat before the photography class and arrived at The Cake Stop with just a few minutes to spare. She decided to do her observing in the classroom.

Jean-Philippe greeted her with a quizzical expression as she walked straight past the coffee machine and the cakes - which sat oozing cream and deliciousness - reproaching her.

"You are *malade?*" asked the barista with mock concern.

"Staying neutral," she whispered. "Seeing what I can learn upstairs." Clutching her notebook, with a boyish grin she shot up the stairs, two at a time.

There was a very subdued air in the room. The buzz from the last class was missing. As was Janice, unsurprisingly. Niamh also wasn't there, and remembering her request she went over to Oliver.

"Niamh is unwell and won't be coming today. She asked me to tender her apologies."

"Ah, er, right, right, thank you, er .." Oliver blinked, looking ever more like an owl in his brown suit with those wispy brown curls sticking out at the sides of his head like owls' ears. "I think there may be a few missing tonight. Sad. Very sad." He cleared his throat and declaimed, "Ladies and Gentlemen. I'm sure you all know by now about the sad loss of one of our students. Naturally her sister is not here tonight." He cleared his throat. "May we all stand for a minute's silence in remembrance of Estelle Carruthers?"

There was a scraping of chairs and shuffling of feet as everyone stood. Tamsin noticed, from her vantage point at the far left corner of the room, that Duncan Hattersley jumped up quickly, while Grace Metcalfe sighed noisily before heaving herself to her feet. Joe Bucket got up stiffly and leaned heavily on the back of the chair in front. The silence was ... not exactly silent - with coughing, a sneeze, someone dropping their spiral-bound notebook with a clatter, and some barely-suppressed giggles from Jessica and Chloe, who seemed quite incapable of standing still.

"Ah, thank you," said Oliver, and everyone sat down again, with throat-clearings and mumblings. There were a few empty seats: the Carruthers sisters naturally, Niamh O'Connor, and, worryingly, Mark Bendick's usual seat was also empty - but at that moment the door opened and in rushed Mark himself, sheepishly apologising for being late. Tamsin felt a flood of relief wash over her, and gave him a secret wave as he found his seat at the other end of the row.

Oliver started the lesson and went through his slides. Knowing how detailed his handouts were, Tamsin kept her notebook and pen on her lap and paid attention to the lesson.

"Today, we're going to look at close-up photography, and specifically portraits. If your interest is landscapes or plants, then you will still learn a lot from this lesson." And Oliver went on to discuss lighting the subject, and angle of shot, with particular emphasis on the distortion you can get with a camera.

"You see, our eyes compensate. If we look up at a tall person, we don't see a big body with a small head. We correct it visually and simply see - a person. The camera has no such skills, and renders what's in front of it." He fished in his pocket and held up a coin. "Do you see a circle?" Most people nodded. Grace sighed again. Joe Bucket squinted and adjusted his glasses on his nose. Oliver tilted the coin so that it was almost flat. "Now what do you see? Is it still a circle?"

There was some foot-shuffling, then Joe said, "That be a circle on its side!"

"That's what it *is!* But in fact, what you're *seeing* is an ellipse!"

He peered round the room for a reaction. The two teenagers were sitting, heads together, scrolling through one of their phones. Mark looked baffled, possibly not knowing the meaning of the word 'ellipse'. Several people nodded.

"We know it's a round coin," Oliver went on, "so that's what we see. And if we're expecting it to look like a round coin in our photo, we will be disappointed!" He grinned impishly.

"Oh!" Tamsin spoke up. "People are always showing me photos of their dogs taken from above! They have a huge head and tiny paws sticking out under their chin - they're not seeing what the camera sees."

"That's absolutely right, er .. Tamsin." Oliver beamed at his star pupil, glad that at least one of them had got the point. "And that's what we're looking at today. How to avoid distortions in close-up photography."

The rest of the lesson was very absorbing to Tamsin. While most of Oliver's examples were portraits of people, he had taken the trouble to show distorted images of plants, landscapes and townscapes, vehicles, food, and animals, so that all his students could relate to the lesson. Gradually the scales fell from the students' eyes, and they got more and more engaged in the teaching. Even the two girls were captivated, and at question time they had lots to ask about ring-lights and eye reflections.

"So your assignment this week will be - close-ups. They can be of anything you like, but I want to see at least one portrait of a person amongst your submissions. The handout details everything you need to remember." He smiled benignly over his round spectacles at his flock of owlets. "I suggest you take at least a hundred pictures over the week with these considerations in mind. Now, let's take a short break before we look over your photos from last week."

Several people went to fetch a glass of water from the back of the room, and, the mood having lifted, were ready to chat with each other. Tamsin joined Mark, who had been accosted by the two girls. "I ain't going near them Hills ever again," Jessica told him. "Nor me neither," agreed Chloe. Tamsin reckoned they had never have been near them at all in the first place - their natural habitat seemed to be shops or maybe night clubs. Mark reassured them, "I'm up there all the time, with the Nighthawks."

"The who?" Jessica gaped.

"The Nighthawks. The mountain bikers. We ride there at night."

"Oo-er," said Chloe, and glancing at her friend they sidled away.

"It would take more than an unexplained death to keep *us* off the Hills, eh, Mark?" Tamsin quipped.

"Right on!" he replied, then leant over and spoke out of the side of his mouth, "and it ain't yet!"

"I'm glad to see you not behind bars," she added quietly. "What did they have you in for?"

Mark blushed to his roots. "Give a dog a bad name, eh? Fortunately I had an alibi for that time. I was working late at *Flying Pedals* - we had a stack of bikes to get ready for the weekend and the other guys were doing overtime too."

"But they kept you in till they'd checked it out?" Tamsin frowned. She knew that many others would have been released while they investigated. "They should know that you've turned over a new leaf by now!"

"They oughta. But they were nice enough. You get to know these coppers .." He brightened up, "and the food was halfway decent!"

Tamsin laughed, "Don't tell your mother!"

They were joined by Lucinda, so they abruptly left the subject. "Wasn't that a fascinating lesson?" she enthused. "It's so important that I don't get any distortion in my botanical drawings."

"I suppose you have to be very precise?"

"Accuracy is vital in a textbook!" At the word 'textbook' Mark drifted away.

"I think I saw you in town the other day," Tamsin suggested.

"Oh yes? I do venture out from my studio from time to time," Lucinda laughed loudly. "When was this?"

"Last Thursday. I was doing our assignment. You were in a shop doorway."

"Would that be the arts supplies shop? I'm always there - they do well out of me! They're very good - they get my paper in *specially*."

"Yes, I think it was. Then you followed Estelle along Graham Road."

"Estelle? She was there? That poor woman! Such an awful thing to happen. You know I've always thought women shouldn't walk the Hills on their own - far too dangerous. You just never know who may be about." She chattered fast. Tamsin could recognise a diversion tactic when she heard one.

The chink of Oliver tapping the projector with his pen cut across Lucinda's chatter. She smiled disarmingly and they returned to their seats. But not before Tamsin noticed a look passing between Duncan and Grace.

Now they came to everyone's homework. Tamsin was only interested in photos taken on Thursday - a still, sunny, day, so these pictures were easily picked out of the otherwise rather grey and breezy week.

Joe Bucket's pictures were taken in the Link, on a rainy day. People were hurrying in and out of shops, hunched over, some carrying umbrellas. "This is a great depiction of people going about their business in the rain - nicely done, Joe. I like the reflections you picked up on the wet road."

"I never knew I done that!" guffawed Joe.

"Then you did it naturally. Well done!" Oliver responded encouragingly.

Jessica and Chloe had produced some interesting photos between them. They used the fashion shop windows to capture their own reflections, with real people walking along the pavement between them and their reflected selves and the mannequins. "This is very imaginative, young ladies!" said Oliver approvingly, pointing out a couple of photos where they could have considered the composition slightly more. In one of their pictures Tamsin was amused to see Charity and Muffin walking up the hill towards The Cake Stop. It must have been Saturday, then.

Duncan had chosen to take photos of the Victorian residential area of Great Malvern. Some of the large old houses had become offices or clinics, and there was plenty of coming and going. It was a windy day, and a group of women chatting on the pavement had to keep sweeping their hair out of their eyes. Not Thursday.

Grace's pictures were next. They were of the lower part of Church Street looking resplendent in the sunshine. One was taken up the hill, and clearly showed Estelle turning into Graham Road.

There was a gasp from the class.

"Sorry!" said Grace loudly. "Sorry - sent these in before I'd heard. Should have told Oliver not to show that one," she neighed.

Oliver, slightly flustered, chose to ignore that and instead turned quickly to one of the other photos and pointed out some possible improvements in the composition.

The class now felt uneasy as the last set of photos went up on the screen. They were Mark's. He'd taken his pictures along the top road, heading towards Malvern Wells, the sun already hidden behind the Hills and the scene in shadow. There were a few people walking to and from town, some with laden shopping bags. On the road just below Rose Bank Gardens, there was a crowd of people looking up and admiring the magnificent Malvern Buzzards sculpture. Behind the group, Tamsin could just see that trolley. There was Estelle, walking away from town - presumably going to meet her murderer.

She said nothing as Oliver enthused over the sculpture and how Mark could have cropped his image to focus more on the relationship between the tourists and the birds. Nobody else appeared to notice what she had seen. She was so absorbed in this image that she failed to hear Oliver wind up the class. Everyone was already up chatting and taking their handouts.

"Are you alright, Tamsin dear?" asked Damaris, at her side.

"Oh, yes, thank you Damaris. Just thinking about who I can do portraits of," she prevaricated, then blushed at her lie.

"I have two sisters who will have to sit for me!" smiled Damaris.

"The *Malvern Mercury* hasn't had much to say about this .. this .. death," she could hear Lucinda saying to Duncan.

"Too busy going on about the petty thefts. Trying to make a mystery out of it," he replied.

"Are they still going on? There's never a dull moment!" Lucinda giggled schoolgirlishly, and joined the exiting crowd.

Tamsin made her way down the stairs in contemplative mood, wishing that the café hadn't long since closed. The sight of Estelle shortly before her death had quite upset her. Right now she could do with a restorative coffee!

CHAPTER TWENTY-THREE

"So I wondered if I could drop by and take some portrait photos of the children?" Tamsin, now fully tanked up with coffee, was talking to Molly the next morning on the phone.

"I'd love that!" said Molly. "I think you'll bring something fresh to the portraits. They won't look like school portraits, I mean. You should see the last ones they did! Cameron looked like an escaped prisoner, and Joe looked cross-eyed."

"I imagine Alex was just a blur!" laughed Tamsin. "Thanks - that's brilliant, Molly. I'm looking forward to this enormously. But don't pitch your expectations too high! I'm only a beginner."

They'd arranged for her to arrive a while after the children had got back from school. "You'll have to wait for them to have some tea," warned Molly. "They're inhuman till they've eaten and shed the worries of the day."

Tamsin's day's worries were confined to two home visits. A second visit to the puppy in Much Marcle she'd had such fun with last week, followed by one in Redmarley for an imported street-dog with a shed-load of issues. It was baffling to Tamsin that people - and usually bliss-fully unaware first-time owners - thought that taking on such a dog would be an easy ride. Love alone was definitely not enough for these troubled and often abused dogs.

"Hey ho," she said to her own peaceful crew, "there's always the possibility they could turn into wonderdogs, like you three!" Banjo sat and looked adoringly at her, his tail swishing on the floor.

She decided that Quiz could accompany her today, so that maybe she could lay a quick track on the way back from Chas's place. So into the *Top Dogs* van went Quiz's tracking harness and line, along with all the home visit gear.

And when she'd completed her home visits and finally arrived in Lower Thatchall, there was an unaccustomed silence when she knocked on the front door. "Wonder if they're in the garden?" she thought, and started round the side of the house - where she was greeted with a harrowing scene of children sobbing and wailing, their fraught mother trying to comfort them at the same time as carrying her baby daughter who was also grizzling.

"What's up?" Tamsin scooped up the crying Joe and kissed his damp cheek. "Where's Cameron?" Then, looking around quickly and noticing the comparative stillness, "Where's Buster?"

Over the wails of Alex and Amanda, Molly said, "I was just fixing their tea when they arrived home. Next thing I knew, there was no sign of Cameron and Buster. We've checked the whole house - I've no idea where he is!" Molly looked as if she was struggling not to join in with the crying. "He's been gone nearly an hour. I've rung Chas - he's on his way, but he'll be at least half an hour."

"Police?" asked Tamsin quietly.

"Chas said to wait till he's back. Cameron's never done anything like this before!"

"Not much goes on with these boys without the others knowing," Tamsin deposited the snivelling Joe on a bench and moved closer to Molly. "What do they say?"

"They've been sworn to secrecy. Absolutely won't say a word - just keep weeping." It's so hard, with Amanda frightened and screaming as well.

"Let me have a go."

She went over and sat on the bench next to Joe who'd been joined by Alex. The youngest boy turned a blotchy face to her. "Joe," she said, "Alex. Mummy and Amanda are really upset. You need to be very grown up. Until Daddy gets here, you're the oldest men."

Alex pulled himself up a bit taller, and wiped his nose on his sleeve.

"Now, I know how important it is to keep secrets. But there are times when we have to think of what's the best for everyone." Tamsin waited for this to sink in. "I know Cameron is a very good boy. He wouldn't do anything naughty on purpose. He's gone off somewhere with Buster. But think of this - supposing he has a fall? Or Buster gets hurt? We can't help him if we don't know where he is!"

Joe began to cry again. "If you've got any idea where he's gone, don't you think it would be very grown-up to tell us?"

Alex and Joe looked at each other. Tamsin pressed her advantage.

"Supposing they're in a car accident? Or fallen down a well?" Tamsin resolved to ease up a bit as Joe was off again. "You're so observant, you boys. Can you just give me a hint of which way he left?"

There was another pause. Alex shuffled in his seat and looked quickly at Joe. Joe looked up at Tamsin under his long lashes, and looking towards the lane leading to the fields beside their house, he tentatively lifted one finger.

"You're a star, Joe, so you are! A very wise decision. Everyone's going to be so pleased with you." And Tamsin jumped up and asked Molly, still trying to comfort her noisy baby, "Where does that lane lead?"

"Off into the fields. As the crow flies it would take you to Hanley Swan. But there are roads ..." Molly looked aghast.

"I'm going to have a hunt. We have to do something! I've got Quiz with me." Molly looked nonplussed as Tamsin called out, "she's a tracking dog!" and ran round to the front to get her dog and her tracking bag, and pull on her wellington boots.

"Come on, Quiz, you're on!" She hopped the dog out of the van. "And this is for real," she whispered.

As she harnessed Quiz up, she called out, "How do I get to the lane?"

"They always scramble over the bank there, just after the stinging nettle patch."

"I've got my phone. I'll let you know what I find. And ring me if he shows up here again." She walked to the gap in the bank, uncoiled the thirty-foot rope line and attached it to Quiz's harness. The dog, hearing the click, immediately put her nose down at the gap, and surged over the bank, already on the scent, the line running through Tamsin's hands till she started to follow her dog.

The lane was occasionally used by tractors, so it wasn't hard to get along, and was fortunately pretty dry. At the end of the lane were two five-bar gates leading into different fields. Tamsin waited while Quiz cast. She seemed to veer between two tracks - presumably one for the boy and one for his dog. Then she made up her mind and surged to the gate on the right. Tamsin climbed over and fed the line through a gap where Quiz was able to slither between the bars. A bit more casting and she picked up speed again. "Great girl, Quizzy," muttered Tamsin, her heart racing.

At the bottom of that field they had to clamber down a dry ditch and through a scrawny hedge. Tamsin was getting scratched but put it out of her mind, thinking instead of the dear small boy and his little dog, who were in such danger.

Suddenly Quiz threw herself to the ground. She'd found something!

Tamsin dropped the line and ran up to look. It was a fresh apple core. She picked it up and looked closely at the bite marks - yes, those were surely a child's ridged front teeth marks! She stowed the find in her bag, congratulated her panting dog and pressed on.

She'd crossed four more fields and could hear the distant roar of traffic on the main road ahead when Quiz found something new. This time it was invisible to Tamsin, but judging from the bitch's behaviour, she felt sure it was where Buster had peed. Onward! Fast!

And, approaching a copse of trees in the centre of a huge barley field, she heard something else - it was Buster barking! Tamsin's heart lifted with relief, then realised there could still be trouble. Quiz looked up from her fixation on the track, gave a single bark, and put her nose down and tracked on. She skirted the perimeter of the copse then halfway round she dived in, trampling over twigs and pushing through clumps of thistles. Buster's bark was louder now.

Then Tamsin saw them. Hallelujah!

"Cameron!" she called. "Buster!" The boy was sitting on the ground amidst the beechmast under the great trees. He looked up and Tamsin could see yet another tear-stained face. Buster ran toward her, wagged his tail at the sight of her and Quiz, then spun round with another bark and ran back to his little master.

Tamsin unclipped Quiz's harness - "I'm so proud of you, Quiz!" - and ran over to see Cameron.

"I hurt my leg," he said slowly, his round eyes looking up at Tamsin as if it was quite normal for them to meet here. "Have you got a plaster, please?"

"Oh Cameron, bless you! Let's have a look." He had a rip on his leg, with a hawthorn embedded in it. "Ouch!" said Tamsin, "That will need tweezers. And that's one thing I don't have with me! Can you walk?"

"I can, but it does hurt. Quite a bit, actually." He screwed up his face.

"Just give me a moment, old thing." Tamsin walked a little away from him. Quiz hesitated for a moment, then lay down next to the boy, knowing where she was needed most. Tamsin smiled as she saw Cameron bury his face in her furry neck, then tapped a message on her phone:

No need for helicopters! Found them. Both safe. I'll get you a map reference.

Then, looking around to work out what road they were near, she used a couple of apps on her phone to get a precise location.

Can Chas get here? It's not far from the road.

She went back to Cameron. "Buster helped us to rescue you, you know. He's a very good dog."

"He's a very, very, good dog," said the little boy, and clasped his thin arm tightly round Buster's neck.

"But tell me Cameron - where were you going?"

"It's our teacher. Miss O'Connor. She's ever so nice. And she's disappeared. I went to find her."

"Disappeared? How do you know?"

"She was off sick yesterday. And she wasn't there again today. And I heard the teachers talking when I went past the Staff Room at break time. They said she'd vanished!"

Tamsin chewed this new information over. What could have happened to mousey Niamh? Was this to do with Estelle's murder? Where did she fit in?

And to Cameron she said, "You can't walk all the way back with that injury. But it's ok, Dad's going to come out with the car. He'll be able to carry you across the fields. You're way too heavy for me!"

Cameron looked relieved.

"I see you brought provisions for your journey?" Tamsin said.

He looked at her in amazement. "I did. I brought an apple and some biscuits. I ate the apple."

"I know," she smiled.

He frowned in puzzlement. "But I still have the biscuits! Want one?"

"I think I will," and Tamsin took a couple of pieces of smashed-up biscuit that Cameron extracted from his pocket. "I have treats for the dogs though, and they both deserve them." She gave Quiz a treat, and gave a handful to Cameron to give Buster. She poured out some water for the dogs from her tracking bag, and gave the bottle to the little boy to refresh himself.

"I wish I could lap from a bowl," he said wistfully.

"Would be good, wouldn't it!"

It was beginning to get dusky. She got up from the ground. "Let's move to the edge of this copse so Dad can see us." Cameron limped after her and sat down heavily when they reached the field. And guessing which direction Chas would arrive from, she hung her pink jacket up in the branch over them.

They didn't have long to wait before she could see branches moving in the hedgerow near the main road. The tall figure of Chas emerged.

"Quiz, Woof!" And Quiz obliged with several barks till Tamsin said "Thank you," then she stopped. On hearing the barks, Chas broke into a run. Tamsin snatched down her coat and waved it above her head. She stepped forward to meet him as he arrived, his face a picture of worry.

"The great explorer's come a bit unstuck."

Chas bent over his errant son, who tried bravely not to cry, and looked at his leg. "We'll soon sort that out, my lad," he said, and scooped the boy up like a fallen leaf and swung him onto his back. Cameron's thin arms gripped round Chas's shoulders, his hands clasped against his Dad's neck. With a sigh he pressed his cheek to his father's head and relaxed.

Tamsin checked she had everything, and deftly attached both dogs to her tracking line. Chas looked over to her and mouthed, "We can't thank you enough."

"I'm so glad I had Quiz with me at the right moment. Between her and Buster, they saved the day."

Chas smiled and led the way to the road and his waiting car, carrying his precious burden on his back.

CHAPTER TWENTY-FOUR

There was great rejoicing when Chas arrived home with Cameron, Tamsin, and two dogs. The other children ran out to the front garden, shouting, "Were you in deadly danger, Cameron?" and "Are you bleeding? Let's see!" and as Chas carried the boy in, Molly buried her face in the two of them and smiled broadly through her tears.

Cameron was sat on the kitchen table while Molly produced tweezers, cotton wool, witch-hazel and a few more home remedies, and set about removing the nasty thorn. There was a rapt audience of his two brothers for this operation, and applause and encouragement from Amanda in her high chair, slapping her tray table with her hands.

Once the little boy was patched up and had had a proper hug from his Mum, the tea they'd all missed earlier was produced. The children were all starving, and ate ravenously. As were the two dogs, who were each given a bone to gnaw.

"Hot chocolate in front of the tv for you lot now," said Molly. "And homework will have to wait. I'll send a note for your teachers tomorrow." The first announcement was received with big grins, and the second with whoops of joy and waving arms and dancing about. Alex's flailing arms managed to clout Joe on the head, but he let it pass in his jubilation. They were both genuinely relieved to have their beloved older brother back.

While Molly made the hot chocolate, Chas drew Cameron aside.

"Can you tell me why you went off, old man?" And seeing Cameron's anxious face, he added, "You're not in trouble. We just need to know what's up."

Cameron relaxed a little and said what he'd told Tamsin - that his favourite teacher seemed to have gone missing and he thought he'd go looking for her.

"That's a really kind thing to want to do, Cameron. And for that I'm proud of you. But you do need to explain to the grown-ups when you get an idea like that. We could have helped!"

"Sorry Dad."

"A lot of people were really worried about you! And isn't it just as well that Tamsin and Quiz found you and we didn't have to call out the police helicopter?"

"I think I'd have liked the helicopter actually .."

"Come on!" laughed Chas, "Let's get you three wrapped up on the sofa with your chocolate. It'll be bedtime soon enough."

And that being done, a quiet fell on the house. Amanda was happily eating and the blare of the television kept the boys amused. To start with they were all cuddled up together on the sofa, but normal service soon resumed, with minor warfare breaking out now and then.

"So what's all this about the teacher going AWOL?" asked Chas.

"I *think* it's to do with the murder," Tamsin began. Both Chas and Molly looked at her with surprise. "You see, Niamh is in the same photography class that I am, and Estelle Carruthers was too. As you can perhaps imagine," she gave a wry smile, "I'm doing a bit of investigating."

"No surprise there!" Chas winked at Molly.

"Well, I went round to see Niamh on Tuesday evening. She said she didn't know the victim - hadn't even noticed her in class - but I honestly didn't believe her. She's very sweet and angelic, and I'm sure she's a lovely junior school teacher ..."

"Cameron is clearly smitten," Molly agreed.

".. but somehow what she was saying didn't ring true. Anyhow, the next day she texted me to say she had a headache and wouldn't be at the photography class and would I give her apologies. I don't know why she told me and not the teacher direct."

Molly nodded. "Apparently she wasn't in again today. There are so few teachers in our little school - Alex was telling me they had to double up some of the classes today because of her being out."

"Can you see why I think there may be a connection?"

"I hope you're not saying she killed this woman?"

Tamsin thought for a moment. "Let's say I'd be really surprised if she had. She's very shy and quiet, but I think that's partly a blind."

"I have to agree with you there," said Chas with feeling. "At the last Parents' Night she struck me as being very astute. She could see exactly what Alex's issues are - and I can tell you there have already been a few teachers in his short school life who didn't understand him at all. Just thought he was naughty."

"So she's perspicacious as well." Tamsin stood up and called Quiz over to her. She looked at her two friends, now beginning to relax again. "Even I can see some things - you're all wrecked and need some peace and quiet." She looked over to Quiz, who dropped her bone, looked at it, at Buster, then trotted over without it. "Don't worry Quizzy old thing, dinner when we get home."

There were more effusive thanks as she made her way out to her van. Tamsin hugged Molly, saying, "Not at all. It was fortunate timing, that's all. And I would still like to try those portraits - I'll give you a buzz tomorrow."

Tamsin didn't realise how affected she was by the excitement of the afternoon till she got home. She fed the dogs, made herself a coffee and subsided into an armchair to think.

And thinking rapidly became dozing. So she got quite a fright when Emerald arrived home from her class and she awoke to find the room in darkness. Opal had been curled up on her lap, and all the excitement from the dogs caused her to leap off, digging her back claws into Tamsin's leg.

"Hey Sleepyhead!" said Emerald, walking in to the living room, switching on the standard lamp, and seeing her bleary-eyed housemate just coming to. "So this is what you do when I'm out! And there was me thinking you were a hard worker."

Tamsin grinned and regaled Emerald with the afternoon's events. Emerald was duly astonished. "Thank God you had Quiz with you! Poor Molly ... So have you eaten?"

"No. I came home and - just flaked out."

"Too much emotion," the yogi nodded her head sagely. "I'll fix you some dinner. Come and keep me company and tell me more." She stood up and pulled the band off her pony tail, shaking out her long blonde hair. "Ok Opal, I'll feed you too, don't worry."

They adjourned to the kitchen.

"Tell me what you thought of Niamh O'Connor," said Tamsin, nibbling some nuts.

Emerald thought hard as she gave the pasta pan a stir. "She comes over as all sweetness and light. But you're right, she was pretending when she said she didn't know who Estelle was."

"I love how you say 'pretending' when you mean 'lying'," Tamsin smirked, and helped herself to a baby tomato. "Gosh, I *am* hungry!"

"She suddenly became more brittle. Too keen to make her point."

"Mmm. 'The lady doth protest too much, methinks'. And then she disappeared." Tamsin waved the tomato in the air. "First feigning a headache, and then, apparently, silence."

"I wonder if anyone's reported her missing? Like the school?"

"That I don't know. But I know who might know!" and she fished her phone out of her pocket to ring Feargal.

Feargal answered quickly. Tamsin could barely hear him against the noise in the background. "I'm covering an RTC on the Worcester Road - two cars and an artic. It's a bad smash - fire engine's here, the works. But no fatalities. I'll get back to you tomorrow morning. We have to catch up anyway."

So they arranged to meet at The Cake Stop the next day.

Tamsin gave a big yawn as she rang off. "That'll be interesting. But right now, I'm going to do this lovely supper justice then stretch out in the living room in front of some undemanding tv."

CHAPTER TWENTY-FIVE

It was a beautiful warm Autumn day as Tamsin and Emerald, with Banjo and Moonbeam trotting along with them, made their way to their favourite café. Quiz was enjoying a well-earned rest back at Pippin Lane. They cut across the Common, keeping to the paths as the dew hadn't yet burned off the grass. The trees were already turning yellow in places, and leaves were gathering in bedraggled heaps where the wind had blown them.

Tamsin couldn't help herself and she took some pictures of the dogs' pink and yellow frisbee floating high over them as they ran for it, hanging in the air apparently above the majestic Malverns towering behind. Then for good measure she turned right round and took some more pictures, catching the haze over the River Severn down in the valley.

"I think I need a reward for yesterday's adventure," said Tamsin, pocketing her phone, her tummy rumbling at the thought of the cake counter.

"Since when did you need an excuse to eat cake?" Emerald grinned, as she wafted along beside Tamsin, her floaty cream dress moving in the light breeze and outlining her long slender body.

"You're right. I wonder what the Furies have produced for us today." She patted her tummy to assuage the rumbles as they went through the big glass door with *The Cake Stop* etched in the glass and got a cheery welcome from Kylie and Jean-Philippe.

"So you have decided to visit us properly today, *hein?*" Jean-Philippe jested as they approached the display of food and the mighty coffee machine.

"Couldn't hold out any longer! Oh my," Tamsin's mouth watered as she looked at the shelves of magnificent baking from the Furies. "I haven't seen that one before?" She pointed to a frothy yellow and white concoction sprinkled with fresh raspberries.

"Ooh, you gotta try that one, Tamsin!" said Kylie, pulling the plate from the shelf. "It's like lemon meringue, only it's made with the lightest of cake, and lashings of cream. Gorgeous! Two slices?" she looked enquiringly at Emerald.

"Go on," Emerald answered. "I can always pass what I don't finish to Feargal. He's a professional plate-cleaner."

"Ah, it'll be nice to see our intrepid reporter again," chirped Kylie, preparing their coffees and tossing a couple of biscuits down for the dogs.

The café was busy already but Jean-Philippe moved the little sofa around so they could sit in the window. He knew how the dogs loved to lie on their pink mats where no-one could tread on them and watch the world go by on the street. And it wasn't long before they saw Feargal striding up the hill towards the café, talking rapidly into his phone.

"Filing a report?" asked Emerald when he eventually joined them, with a tray laden with food.

"Latest update on that smash last night."

"Nasty," Emerald grimaced.

"It's a tricky stretch of road. They need to do something with it - put in some calming measures or something. Anyway, it's all clear now and the people aren't too badly injured."

"That's a relief," Emerald felt able to take another spoonful of her cake.

"So, what's the latest?"

While he ploughed through his toasted sandwich and cake - this time he'd chosen a slice of Bakewell Tart, its frangipane filling oozing out under the multitude of flaked almonds - Tamsin filled him in on yesterday's events.

"These dogs of yours are the goods! Cameron's a great little lad. Glad he's ok." he said, then looked sadly at his empty plates and mug. "I needed that - let's have another round of coffees," and he gave Kylie a wave, pointing at their mugs. "I've got some info for you, though, on those three names."

He pulled out his phone and located his notes. "Duncan Hattersley. Was a clerk in local government in Dudley. Retired to Great Malvern three years ago, to the house his grandfather lived in. Grandfather big noise in Malvern architectural circles, and adorned his house with strange carvings."

"Oh, is that that big Victorian house round the back of Priory Park? I had a session in one of those big houses once with a barking Dachshund. We recorded him when the owners were out. He hardly made a sound - fussy neighbours, that was all. Wonder if Duncan was one of them? The owners were delighted ... Anyway, I noticed a house opposite with statues and ornamental gables and so on."

"That sounds like the place. He belongs to the local architectural society, preserving Malvern's heritage, that kind of thing. Otherwise, not much is known about Mr. Hattersley."

As she saw Kylie appearing with a tray of coffees, Tamsin scooped the last of the froth from her mug and offered her finger to the dogs to lick. Emerald and Feargal were busy for a moment clearing space on the table, Feargal waving his card over Kylie's machine, then they resumed their conversation.

"Thanks Feargal old bean! Ok, how about Grace Metcalfe? She's a local bird, the *Mercury* must have more on her?"

"Yes, she's been up at Leigh Sinton for ever. Well-known amongst the horsey set. But not well-loved."

"That figures," Tamsin thought of how Grace had treated her stable girl.

"Hard as nails, they imply. Been some jiggery-pokery over winning competitions. But I think that goes on quite a lot."

"Pretty cutthroat business, it seems," Emerald piped up.

"I have the impression from veiled remarks I found, that she's pretty forthright. Nothing stands in her way."

"Interesting," Tamsin murmured. "Forthright is usual a polite way of saying bossy."

"Or rude," Emerald added succinctly.

"You're not wrong," Tamsin nodded.

Feargal referred to his notes again. "Now, the last one, Niamh O'Connor. She arrived here two years ago. She was teaching in Birmingham previous to that. Did her teacher training in Ireland - somewhere in Kerry. That's where she comes from. It's down in the Southwest of Ireland. Gets all the weather from the Atlantic I believe. Touristy area."

"Oh yes - it's very beautiful!" interjected Emerald. "My mother took me there for a holiday once, years ago. We had a gypsy caravan with a horse. He was called Jack! I remember that clearly - big black carthorse with shaggy feet. The Ring of Kerry," she said dreamily. "It's got fabulous views, but for a lot of the year you can't see your hand in front of your face for the drizzle."

"Well, that's where Niamh O'Connor comes from. She seems fairly unremarkable. Couldn't find out anything particular about her. But she has been reported missing. By the school, it seems. And because of a possible connection with this live murder investigation, they've got an All Ports Alert out for her."

"In case she bolts back to Ireland?" asked Emerald.

Feargal nodded, "I guess so."

"So the police are taking it seriously? But I'm not sure any of that gets us any further. Can't see a connection to Estelle Carruthers there at all. She wasn't an architecture buff so far as I know. She had nothing to do with horses."

"She *was* a hill-walker though," Emerald reminded them. "I wonder if she's been walking in Ireland? Lots of hills in Kerry!"

"Perhaps we should talk to the grieving sister again. Hey, Banjo, what's up?" Banjo had sat up and was growling softly. They followed his gaze and saw - Duncan Hattersley! He was staring at the dog disapprovingly from the edge of the wide pavement. "Talk of the devil! It's ok, Banjo, you may ignore him," and she distracted the dog with another lick of milk froth.

"Maybe he disapproves of dogs in cafés," said Feargal.

"Or dogs at all," said Tamsin with gritted teeth. "Thing is, Banjo is a great judge of character. He's never been proved wrong."

"So *you* can see something bad in Duncan, can you?" Emerald stroked the collie's head approvingly. He looked up at her with his clear blue eyes and softly opened his mouth into the smile reserved for his very special people.

"Perhaps we should do an identity parade for Banjo, so he can pick out the baddies for us!" laughed Feargal. "Would save us a lot of time!"

Tamsin smiled as she pictured this, then drank her coffee distractedly. "I have Puppy Class this afternoon, but I fancy fitting in a couple of things."

"Yes?" Her audience waited expectantly.

"I want to talk to Janice again. Would you like to come with me, Em? She responded so well to Charity the other day, rather than me clodhopping about all over her feelings!"

"Sure, I'll come. I'd be interested to meet her."

"And the other thing?" asked Feargal.

"I'm going to take my sniffer dogs up Midsummer again. I think there just may be more to find. If Estelle hid things there once, it's likely she did it other times. If we work on the hypothesis that she'd gone a bit bats and was showing kleptomaniac tendencies, she would need to get rid of the goods somehow - as she didn't actually want them."

"And supposing our other theory?" This from Feargal. "That she was deliberately stealing things of no value to conceal stealing something of actual value. That she wanted for some reason."

"Perhaps to deprive the owner of .. the thing?" asked Emerald.

"Possibly, Emerald. There are all sorts of reasons she may have been doing it. But yes, Tamsin - that sounds like a good plan. When will you go?"

"No time like the present!" Tamsin jumped up and the dogs scrambled to their feet. "I'll go and fetch Quiz - her nose is in great working order this week!"

She packed up the pink dog beds and looked about her to see if she'd forgotten anything. "Want a lift home, Emerald?"

Emerald glanced at Feargal who smiled softly back at her. "Oh," she said, "I still have this coffee to finish ..."

Tamsin knew when not to interfere. "See ya later, kiddo! I'll pick you up from Pippin Lane after Puppy Class. Actually all those puppies always put me in such a mellow state, perhaps I won't be so heartless with Janice!" She shouldered her bag, gave Jean-Philippe a wave and left the café.

CHAPTER TWENTY-SIX

The wind of the last few days had dropped a little. It had been just a breeze down in the town, but up here, on the top of the Malvern Hills, any breeze always became a wind! The sun was low in the sky, it being early October, and the patchwork of fields below were sparkling, lush and green, the mountains in Wales dark on the horizon. More leaves - yellow, yellow and green, and some orange ones - swirled about helplessly where the wind took them.

Tamsin pulled her woolly hat down over her ears and all three of her dogs trudged up the steep approach to Midsummer Hill from the car park and reached the top, at the iron age fort. As they walked alongside the ditch and bank which signified the outer perimeter of the fort, she paused for a moment to think of the people who used to live here - back in the Iron Age.

There had been two hundred houses within these ramparts, she had learnt, home to almost two thousand people. Astonishing to think that three thousand years ago this empty landscape was busy with activity all day long! She crossed the long mound in the centre of the ramparts and said to Moonbeam, "You'd have loved this - this was a specially-built rabbit warren in the Middle Ages when people prized rabbit almost as much as you do!" As she reached the scrub and small trees at the quarry edge of the fort she added, as Moonbeam skipped over behind her friends to start exploring the undergrowth, "Mind you, you'd have been put to death if you'd taken one," for killing a rabbit had carried the death penalty up until the 1800s.

How life changed over the centuries! And here she was in the 21st Century with her working dogs, looking for the detritus of a slightly demented spinster of this parish. It brought a smile to her lips.

"Find!" she exhorted her sniffer dogs, "Where's it gone? Where's it gone?!" She made her way round the ramparts, directing the dogs into the more accessible areas of growth, using her Search hand signal. "This bracken really needs cutting back," she informed them as she stumbled through the dense growth. "We need Joe Bucket up here!" She got a bit near to the old quarry at one stage, and looked down the steep drop at the lake that had formed at the bottom, fed, so it was said, by one of the many springs on the Hills. She called the dogs well away.

After a long stretch of tramping she checked the hour. "Look at the time! Puppy Class is approaching. We'd better finish up here. Pity we didn't find anything, eh Quiz?"

But next to a big clump of blackberries with insects buzzing in and out of the branches, Banjo had stiffened. He was peering into the tangle of brambles. When he found a person in his Search and Rescue duties he would bark to alert his handler. But this was not a person he'd found ...

"Whatcher got, Banjo?" Tamsin trotted over to look over the dog's head. It was so dark inside the clump that she turned on her phone torch to scan, and yes! There was something. She trod on the brambles to make a space to reach in. Another plastic carrier bag! Another *heavy* carrier bag.

"You're a genius, Banjo, so you are!" She ruffled the collie's mane as she heaved the bag onto the grass, using the back of her hand to lift the bag open to peep inside.

At first she couldn't make out what she was looking at, then realised she was looking at the top of the head of a small stone statue.

"No wonder the bag's so heavy! I'd love to get this out and have a proper look," she told Banjo, who was still beside her, admiring his find. "But we have to avoid smudging pawprints," she grinned.

It would have been just about possible for Estelle to drag her trolley up here. It would have been hard to carry the deadweight of the statue without it.

"It has to be Estelle," she assured Moonbeam and Quiz, who had joined them to look curiously at the find, disappointed that no food seemed to be involved. "What's more, I haven't got a trolley, so I'm going to have to carry this down." Clearly the plastic bag was only a wrapping and wouldn't bear the weight of the statue. So Tamsin took off her jacket and, tying its sleeves round her shoulders, made a kind of papoose with it and a couple of dog leads, so she could carry the statue back to the van without damaging any evidence.

"Let's get you lot home. I have to get my Puppy Class gear and get going." And with a light heart she started back down the hill, one hand supporting her burden, glad that it was down she was going, and not up. Loading everyone into the van, she took her prize back to Pippin Lane and switched dogs for puppy class bags.

As ever, the class was a delight! Tamsin enjoyed stopping people barking commands at their baby dog, and instead showing them how to get willing compliance without any shouting at all. She loved to see the scales fall from their eyes as they discovered a far nicer way to interact with their new family member, shedding the military ideas they'd seen from television "trainers". As always they regaled her with stories about how clever their puppy was as they left the class. So she was in great good humour when she arrived home to collect Emerald.

"We have a couple of errands to run on the way, I'm afraid - and yes please, I'd *love* a coffee before I go. I've had an exciting time up on the Hill!" and she told Emerald all about Banjo's find.

"What are you going to do with it?"

"Police station. But before I hand it over, I want to take a closer look. I thought if I rested it against a cushion I could pull the bag open enough to see it."

"Right you are! I'll take a picture of it for you while you hold the bag open. Won't be up to your standard though," giggled Emerald.

Tamsin brought in the bag and they managed to get a better look at it without damaging anything. "What a charming piece!" said Tamsin.

"It looks like some mediaeval saint or something,"

"But it's much later than that. Looks to me like a Pre-Raphaelite vision of the Middle Ages. If I'm right, this could be valuable!"

"Pre-Raphaelites - they were in the 1800s, weren't they?"

"Yes, five hundred years after the Middle Ages. They saw that time very much through rose-tinted spectacles. They rejected the popular art of the Victorian era." She tilted her head from one side to the other. "This is a fine piece, I believe."

"So we're handing this in to the police. Will you tell them where you got it?"

"Oh yes, I have the co-ordinates. I can pinpoint the spot for them."

"And what's the other visit? You said a couple of errands."

"You know what we were saying about Duncan's house this morning? I'm wondering if that's where this artwork came from. So I want to have a look."

"Discreetly?"

"Very! If it did come from that house .. well, that changes things - a lot!"

CHAPTER TWENTY-SEVEN

Tamsin and Emerald drove slowly along the road where Duncan lived. Emerald had her phone at the ready to take photos, and was keeping it low below the window so it wouldn't be seen. She rested her arm on the door frame and adjusted the phone to peep over it. It was getting late and the streetlights were already on. There was a light visible in the hallway of Duncan's house, but they couldn't tell if he was at home. So after pausing for a moment at the top of the driveway so that Emerald could take some pictures - contorting herself to get photos of the corners of the house, behind the tall hedge - Tamsin made a big play of pointing to the house over the road, and crossing to pull into the drive of the Dachshund people.

Emerald flipped quickly through the photos before they got out. "Look, there are alcoves between the ground floor windows, and they all have statues in - except for this one at the far end on the corner."

"That'll be it! Let's see if Bertie's owner is in," and Tamsin led the way purposefully up to the front door, without looking back at the house opposite.

Bertie was most definitely in, and announced his presence in no uncertain terms when Tamsin pulled the rope of the old-fashioned bell by the front door. Bertie's owner was delighted to see her and welcomed them both in.

"Yvonne, hello - this is my friend Emerald. Bertie - lovely to hear you in such fine voice!" Tamsin bent down to ruffle Bertie's wirehaired head. "And who's your friend?" A slightly smaller version of Bertie appeared shyly from the living room.

"This is Percy!" Yvonne explained. "We were having such fun with Bertie that we thought a friend would be nice for him. He's nearly a year old now - and everything you taught us to do with Bertie worked wonders with Percy. He's ever so good!"

"Glad to hear it - hi Percy." Tamsin squatted down to greet the shyer dog. "You'll have to come to our *Top Dogs* Christmas Party!" After all these extended greetings, they were ushered into the large living room.

"Bed now," said Yvonne, and the two wirehaired sausage dogs ran to their beds and lay down.

"That's impressive!" said Emerald appreciatively. "I'm used to it with Tamsin's dogs, but a lot of people would be amazed to see it."

"I tell you, those lessons were invaluable. Now, what can I do for you? I'm sure you don't have time for social calls, Tamsin, between your school, your newspaper column, and your *detecting*." Yvonne grinned impishly.

"You've got me," Tamsin laughed. "I'll be straight with you - it's like this. We think there may have been some of that pilfering you'll have read about in the *Mercury,* at the house opposite you. I wondered if you'd seen anything odd - say in the last couple of weeks?"

"I don't spend much time looking out of these windows at the front, I'm afraid. I'm always in the kitchen or gardening when I'm at home."

Tamsin's shoulders sagged.

"But I can do better than that!"

Tamsin perked up.

"I have CCTV. Did you not notice the cameras when you arrived?"

"I didn't!"

"They've disguised them rather nicely. In fact I have to shin up a ladder every year to cut back the Wisteria so that they can see out."

Tamsin was on the edge of her seat. "And would you have footage from the last two weeks?" she asked eagerly.

"Let's go and have a look," and Yvonne led the way to a study off the entrance hall. On the desk was a large screen. Yvonne pulled up the chair and opened an app on the computer. Tap tap, she went, and waggled the mouse about. "Ummm," she said. She picked the camera pointing down her drive, directly at Duncan Hattersley's house. "Here we go!" She pointed to the date on the screen. "When do you want to start?"

"Can we go backwards from, say, Thursday at about 7?"

Some more taps and twiddles and Yvonne said, "We can fast forward through an hour at a time, if you like."

"Sounds good - would you like to leave us to it so you can get on with something else?"

"I'm curious! I'll get you started anyway. By the time you get back to last week I'll probably have lost interest." She got up from the chair to make space for Tamsin, drew up another for Emerald, then leant on the back of it to watch.

So they got started, viewing the film an hour at a time, highly speeded up. "There's Duncan going out." Yvonne slowed the recording to normal speed and pointed out the time. "Half past five."

Tamsin nodded thoughtfully, and made a note in her phone. "Let's keep going."

It was true it was pretty boring in the main. They watched the whole of Thursday while it was light. Then Wednesday, then Tuesday. Duncan went in and out. Deliveries were made. The sun rose. The sun set. Nothing of interest. They worked their way back to the week before. Tamsin stretched, then leant forward to her task again and reached Wednesday.

"At least you can skip the early evening," suggested Emerald.

"You're right. There's a couple of hours we can miss."

"You're clearly up to something," Yvonne looked enquiringly at Tamsin. "But no, I won't ask. Here's an earlier chunk of Wednesday."

"This is utterly fascinating!" said Emerald, pointing to the screen. "There's Duncan going out at ... half past eleven."

"And here's Estelle coming in, ten minutes later."

"Wow," breathed Yvonne.

"We can't see the far end of the house, more's the pity," said Emerald, as they watched Estelle disappear behind the hedge. "And here she is again! It took her fifteen minutes."

"And just look how she's having to heave that trolley over the bumps in the pavement." Tamsin turned to Yvonne. "You're a brick, Yvonne. Can you keep these tapes somewhere, in case they're needed later?"

"They keep automatically for a month. But I can mark them anyway." She narrowed her eyes. "This is to do with that woman who was found dead on the Hills, isn't it."

"It is. It confirms something we kinda knew."

"Or guessed at, really," said Emerald.

"Guessing is a big part of it," Tamsin gave her crooked smile. "Don't mention this to anyone, will you?"

Yvonne drew her finger across her lips. "Allow me to show you out," she grinned.

When they got out to the front of the house, accompanied by both dachsies, now accustomed to their visitors and curious about them, Tamsin put on another of her acts. She winked to Yvonne and called out loudly from beside the van, "Be sure you work on that trick for the Christmas party! Percy will do it really well now."

"Just in case .." she muttered to Emerald as they backed out of the drive. "But I don't think he's in - not at the front of the house anyway."

"Police now?"

"Police now." Tamsin put the van into first gear and pulled away.

CHAPTER TWENTY-EIGHT

As they drove down to the police station, Emerald said, "I wonder how observant your Hattersley fellow is. I mean, when did he notice the theft?"

"*Did* he notice the theft?"

"That's a point. Maybe someone else knew about it."

"Not that we could see on that CCTV footage. There was no-one else around."

".. *that we could see,*" repeated Emerald.

"You're right. We couldn't see anyone else. That doesn't mean they weren't there." She drummed her fingers on the steering wheel while they waited behind a bus at the bus stop. "I teach my dogs to keep searching till they've covered all the ground. Quiz takes this to extremes and will keep searching till she finds it."

"Then has to be called off?"

"Yep. She was twenty minutes finding her frisbug in the winter once - it had slid underneath the snow and was quite invisible. I'd never have found it. But we're not going to be called off." She started moving forward again. "We're going to keep searching till we find this answer!" And she pulled up outside the police station.

The Desk Sergeant was in expansive mood today, and was happy to rib Tamsin over her delivery. "More rubbish?" he grinned, as he located the right form on his screen.

"More rubbish. Felt Inspector Hawkins might appreciate it," Tamsin beamed. The Sergeant took all the details, including the map reference for where the statue had been found. She explained that her fingerprints would be on the bag, but that she had taken care not to touch the piece of art.

"And we've got your fingerprints on file, I'm guessing?"

"Oh yes. You have all arch criminals' fingerprints on file, don't you?" she quipped, as she turned to leave with a grin.

Emerald was waiting for her in the van, where she had sensibly opted to remain. "What did they have to say?"

"Not a lot. I'm presuming they know the thief was also their victim? It's up to them to work it out ...

"You're not worried the killer will strike again?"

"My feeling is that Estelle's death was related to something Estelle was doing. Not that we have an axe-wielding lunatic on the loose. Let's go and see what Janice has to say."

Janice looked pale and drawn when she opened the door to them. She peered at Emerald, then at Tamsin. "Oh, it's you. You brought a different friend." She stood back from the door and ushered them in.

"Yes, this is Emerald - the calming influence in my life! I wanted to see how you were bearing up and .. thought she might calm you too. I mean," she added hastily, "you're going through a lot."

Janice drew out a chair from the kitchen table and almost fell into it. "It's been so awful. And you know, no-one wants to talk to me! Maybe they think I need time alone." She pulled a tissue from her pocket and started to shred it between her two hands. "I have the rest of my life to be alone!"

Emerald took her cue, and leant forward to touch her hand. "We understand," she said quietly. "Tell me a little about your sister."

And as before, this became a soothing exercise for Janice as she went back into her memory of her sister Estelle.

"What did she enjoy doing?" Emerald urged her.

"She loved walking. She'd walk as the day was long." Janice's eyes glazed over and she smiled. "We used to go on walking holidays. So she could walk some more."

"In England? Or abroad?"

"Mostly England - but we did go to France one year, and to Ireland once. The Ring of Kerry. Very beautiful - when you can see it!" she gave a light laugh.

"Oh, I went there for a holiday once!" exclaimed Emerald. "It *was* beautiful - when you could see it, you're right! We were slumming it in a horse-drawn caravan. Bet you were more comfortable?"

"We just stayed in B&Bs. Nothing special."

"Were they good?"

"They were fine, as rural B&Bs go." She sighed, "But Estelle found plenty to complain about, I'm afraid ... she often did. She got quite rude with one or two of the ladies."

"Perhaps she was tired?" Emerald soothed her.

Tamsin, having noted the Kerry connection most carefully, tried another tack. "How about here in little ole England? Do you walk much on the Hills?"

"Oh yes! We'd walk there a lot. Got to know all the nooks and crannies, all the wells, and springs, where the bridlepaths are so we could avoid them ..."

"You don't like horses?"

"I'm a bit nervous of them. But Estelle had a bad experience once - with a rider, not the horse. She thought the rider was bossy and overbearing and wanted to avoid horses after that."

Tamsin thought of her friend Sara in Bishop's Green, who she'd first met over that business with the bow and arrows. She had a beautiful mare called Crystal, and no-one would ever describe her as bossy or overbearing. It seemed to fit with Estelle's character, that she should tar everyone with the same brush.

"Gosh! That wasn't on our Hills, surely?" Emerald's eyes were round.

"It was, actually. Someone who's often up there, with different horses." She looked at Tamsin. "You'd know her. She's in the photography class too."

Tamsin feigned astonishment. "You don't mean Grace Metcalfe?"

"The same. Very grumpy person. Seems to think that everyone is a lackey who can be ordered about."

"Ooh, I'll be careful to avoid her! Tell me, will you be coming back to the class? I mean, it could be a really good thing to focus on."

Emerald joined in, "I'm sure you could take some lovely photos of the Malverns. Kind of commemorate all the places you went with your sister."

"And we'd love to see you back there. Think of the exhibition! Your photos would be on the walls of The Cake Stop."

"That is a nice thought, dear. Thank you." Janice was hesitant, and Tamsin got to her feet.

"Do come!"

"You know, I think I might," Janice smiled bravely up at her. "I'll make it a memorial project."

So they took their leave. And once back in the van and heading home, Tamsin said, "Now, that was all *very* interesting!"

"It sure was! Estelle had had a run-in with Grace - who we know to be bossy and grumpy - and she *may* have come across Niamh in Kerry."

"I think it's quite likely. In rural areas like that - firmly on the tourist trail - every other house does B&B. It's how they survive."

"So, perhaps Niamh's mother ran a B&B. And she was one of the objects of Estelle's complaints?" Emerald waved out of the window as she saw one of her yoga students walking along the road.

"It seems Estelle was very liberal in her complaining."

"An old bat."

"And some people have a very low tolerance for old bats. Grace is grumpy with everyone, it seems. And positively nasty to people she considers beneath her, like her stable girls."

"I can imagine Niamh coming from a modest countryside background. She's all sweetness and light. But if her mother was under attack, I think she may become something else entirely!"

"A Mama Bear?"

"I think so. *I'm* a quiet person, but I won't stand for injustice. If someone attacked my crazy mother, I'd be right there! That's why it's so easy to join you in these investigations."

"You're a most welcome addition to the team!"

"The Malvern Hills Detectives, fighting for justice and right! Here, you don't think that bang on the head was caused by a horse's hoof, do you?"

Tamsin thought for a moment. "I asked Maggie that, but she was sure it was the stone in the car park. Anyway, how would Estelle have got there?"

"Of course. Forgot that. It's hard to keep track of all these details."

"I think we're doing pretty well." Tamsin pulled into the drive in Pippin Lane and pulled up the hand-brake. "I'm wondering if there's any news of Niamh. It's beginning to be a bit worrying."

"It is. Let's ask Feargal if he knows anything."

"Good plan," but my first priority is ..

"Coffee! And food!"

"You know me too well," Tamsin chuckled as she locked the van and unlocked the back door, where she was instantly enveloped in a furry tornado of excitement.

CHAPTER TWENTY-NINE

Once she was coffee-ed up, the dogs and cat were fed and watered, and Emerald set about concocting some tasty food, Tamsin buzzed a text to Feargal. His reply came straight away.

Can I come over? Got some info for you.

She replied in the affirmative, and called to Emerald, "Better double up on the rations!"

"I guess that means we're getting a visitation?" Emerald looked happy at the prospect, and started chopping more vegetables, humming as she worked.

It was still twilight, and Tamsin went out to the garden to have some restful games with her dogs. She glanced up at the dark blue shape of the Malvern Hills above her, now with mist beginning to swirl down the slopes amidst the trees, giving the Hills an other-worldly appearance.

The garden wasn't all that big, but she was able to work on her "Go" cue. She set Banjo up beside her, said "Go!" and once he was running straight ahead, threw her purple hoop so it floated over his head for him to chase and catch as it rolled along the grass.

After a couple of throws she was tugging on the hoop with the excited grey collie, and said, "You're getting good at this, Banjo old bean. Time for Quiz to have a go. Here Quizzy!" and she repeated the performance a few times with Quiz. Quiz was not as fast as the younger dog, but enjoyed the game nonetheless, and was very good at staring ahead waiting for her cue to Go.

"Now for you Moonbeam." The little dog danced on her long thin legs and shot ahead fast when Tamsin called "Go!" She caught the hoop - but it was a bit big for her to manage, so she came running back on three legs, with one leg poking through the hoop she held in her mouth. Tamsin was laughing loudly at this sight, when she heard Feargal's car pull up at the front of the house, and calling the panting dogs, she went in.

"That looked like fun," said Emerald. "Grub's nearly ready. Would you like to do the glasses of water, Tamsin?"

Feargal came through the door, to be mobbed by an excited trio of dogs, for he was one of their favourite people. "Sure! Hi, Feargal. Were you feeling a bit hungry?" she gave a crooked smile.

"Hi, old thing," he grinned back. "If I'm doing all this work for you, isn't the labourer worthy of his hire?"

"It's not as if I'm making money at this," she grumbled. "It's the joy of righting wrongs. That alone should be your reward!"

Emerald clattered some plates. "While you're busy bickering, Muggins here has got the dinner ready. Fancy helping yourselves? Then we can sit in the living room and eat off our laps."

"Brilliant! Thank you," said Feargal eagerly, and they all loaded their plates, Tamsin adding hers to a tray bearing a jug and three glasses.

It was tagliatelle with courgettes and peas in a herby sauce that Emerald had quickly magicked up out of nowhere, and they all ate hungrily in silence for a while.

"You're a mean cook," Feargal cleared the last strands of pasta off his plate. "That was lovely!"

"Thanks, Em. I think I'd fade away without you here."

"Really? Wouldn't cake keep you alive?"

"Point taken. I'd expand without limits, not fade away." She collected their plates, topped up their glasses and said, "Right. Where are we?"

"The statue?" prompted Emerald.

"The *statue!* Yes, we have news about the statue." She described the goings-on at Duncan's house to Feargal, as seen on her Dachshund owner Yvonne's cameras. "So we didn't see anyone watching, but we did see Estelle going in to Duncan's house and coming out a good bit later. With that confounded trolley of hers."

"And we did see that a statue appeared to be missing from one of the alcoves on the house frontage," Emerald added.

"It's circumstantial, but it looks pretty definite that Estelle took it."

"Pretty much. And *then* - this is the exciting bit! - today I went up Midsummer Hill with my search dogs. And we found the statue! Just the right size to fit that alcove, and judging from Emerald's photos, very much in the same style as the others."

"Your dogs are amazing! They searched the whole of Midsummer Hill and found the treasure trove!"

"They did," said Tamsin. "They were brilliant. Look at them now, all sleeping the sleep of the just." She gazed proudly at Quiz on her soft bed, Moonbeam next to Emerald on the sofa, and Banjo stretched out on the hard floor, beside another soft bed.

"Can I see this statue?" asked Feargal.

"It's already in the hands of the rozzers. Took it down to the station this afternoon. It's a nice piece, in the pre-Raphaelite style. Can you show Feargal the pictures you took, Em?"

He scrolled through the photos. "Hmm. I don't know much about art. But you say it's good?" He tapped his fingers on his knee as he thought. "Know what? This Hattersley geezer is an architecture buff, isn't he?"

Tamsin and Emerald nodded.

"I'm going to ask for an interview with him, for the paper. About the architecture of Malvern or something."

"Great idea!"

"Then I can get talking to him and find out all about this statue!"

"Brilliant! Do you think you can get this done quickly?"

"Oh yes. Fast-moving paper is the *Malvern Mercury*," he grinned. "I'll tell him it's urgent that we catch Monday's paper. Should be able to see him tomorrow."

"What I'd like to know is when he noticed the statue missing - if indeed he noticed it at all. I wouldn't put him down as a great actor from what I've seen of him. Should be easy to tell if he's lying."

"I'm on it."

"That's one thing in hand. Do you have any news about our missing teacher?"

"Ah yes. Sorry, should have told you that first. She did go back to Ireland. The *Gardaí* picked her up. She's being shipped back here for questioning."

"Goodness! I wonder what caused her to flee?" Emerald frowned.

"Something must have panicked her alright. I really don't see her as a murderer though."

"But you never know ..." Feargal injected a note of realism. "The shyest, most mouse-like people have harboured horrible secrets."

"Is true. At least I'll have good news for Cameron when I go round tomorrow. She may be up for a capital charge, but for now she's safe and well."

"But you won't be saying that to the children?" Emerald's mouth fell open.

"Don't worry, I wouldn't dream of it. Just that she's been found. He can stop worrying."

"For now."

CHAPTER THIRTY

Tamsin spent a wonderful morning at Chas and Molly's home, taking photo portraits of the children. She was trying hard to remember everything Oliver had taught them about the light, and chose a soft diffused light from an east-facing window to illumine their soft childish features. Nothing harsh needed here!

The boys thought this was all hysterically funny - especially trying to make their brother giggle when he was meant to be relaxing his face. So Molly turfed them out into the garden with Buster and their football, only to come in when it was their turn.

Tamsin found that chatting calmly to the boys about their favourite thing produced some interesting expressions. And gradually she found the best angle for the light to catch their eyes and bring the images to life.

When she was done, having taken some pictures of Amanda who looked delightful on waking from her nap, with tousled hair, dimpled cheeks and a gurgly smile, she showed the photos round to them all.

Molly was thrilled, and picked some out for special mention. "May I have copies of these? Could you send them to me? Oh - should I pay you?"

"Absolutely yes to sending them to you, and absolutely no to payment!" Tamsin replied, feeling flattered anyway. "I'm really grateful for you for being my studio for the morning."

"That's a gorgeous one of Joe," Molly tilted her head from one side to the other as she smiled dotingly over the photo.

"Mine's better!" protested Alex, pushing in beside her. "That one of Cameron with Buster is good though." He conceded as he looked up at Tamsin with shining eyes.

Cameron was just reaching the age of self-awareness. Tamsin had had to work to stop him posing during his session, but he was certainly posing now, as he considered himself not only the oldest, but the most handsome of the three boys.

"I'm pretty pleased with a lot of them. I hope the teacher thinks the same!"

"Talking of teachers," said Molly, "I'm so glad that you could put our minds at rest over Cameron's teacher."

"Er, yes. Yes, it's good that they've found her."

"Will she be at school on Monday?" Cameron was keen to know.

"I don't know. Maybe she needs a little time off to feel better again. Now - what's Buster up to with that ball?" She diverted their attention so the subject could be changed, and they all hared out to the garden shrieking to start their game again.

After leaving their home, Tamsin pointed the *Top Dogs* van towards Hanley Swan. "May be worth seeing if she's home again," she thought as she drove. "After all, with all that song and dance on Thursday, I'm involved in this!"

And she was pleased to find Niamh was home. She opened the front door a crack and peeped out gingerly, but relaxed when she saw who it was.

"I was worried you may be a reporter or something," she said, as she led the way up to her room.

"No, I just wanted to see if you were ok. I don't know if they told you what happened on Thursday, with Cameron?"

"No?" Niamh looked startled. "Is he alright?"

"He is." (No thanks to you, Tamsin thought bitterly.) And she told Niamh the story.

She was suitably mortified. "I had no idea he'd take it to heart so. Bless him - he's a lovely little boy. Thank goodness you found him ok!"

"Indeed. They would have had to get the helicopter out ... So tell me, Niamh, what was all that about?"

"The police have been asking that," she sighed. "Have to investigate thoroughly in the case of an unexplained death, they told me. I really didn't mean to cause all this trouble!" Her eyes glistened.

"So tell me."

Niamh took a deep breath, sighed, dropped her shoulders, and began. "Estelle Carruthers was a nasty woman. Shortly after my father died Mammy started doing Bed and Breakfast. She had to make ends meet, and she needed something to be doing to take her mind off ... Dad. She spent ages getting everything just right, and passing the inspections and all that. And one of our earliest guests was those two sisters."

Tamsin nodded encouragingly.

"Estelle found fault with everything. Just everything. Nothing was right. And Mammy was mortified! After all the work she'd put in ... She nearly abandoned the whole project on the spot. I tried to comfort her, but I was only young myself. And to cap it all, after they'd left we found that the little Belleek jug Dad had given Mammy as a souvenir of their honeymoon in Donegal was missing. She was so upset! Of course we couldn't prove it was them. But when Estelle showed up at the photography class I recognised her right away." She turned her tear-streaked face to Tamsin, "Her face was etched in my memory."

"I can understand that," Tamsin said with feeling.

"So there was this spate of pilfering going on. And seeing Estelle again at the same time, I just put two and two together. It had to be her who'd stolen Mammy's jug. I hated her so much." She gritted her teeth. "So when she was found dead I was overwhelmed with guilt. I would have killed her myself - if I could ever do such a thing, which I'm sure I couldn't. I was shocked by the strength of my feelings, and what could have actually happened if I'd let it. So I ran away. I went back to my Mam. And do you know what?" she appealed to Tamsin. "She'd almost completely forgotten the whole episode. She'd forgiven the woman long ago, and I hadn't."

Tamsin nodded. "Does your mother still run the B&B?"

"She does. It took a while to build her confidence up again. And she'd managed to put it all out of her mind. I needed a bit of time to get over it - and then the *Gardaí* turned up and told me I was wanted for questioning in connection with Estelle's murder."

"That must have been shocking!"

"It was. But my Mam is a tower of strength. And she has great trust in the justice system. 'Just tell them the truth!' she told me."

"And - did you?"

"I did. I thought they'd never believe me." She sniffed and blew her nose on the damp tissue she'd been twisting in her hands. "But they did."

"So you can follow your Mam's example and put it all out of your mind now, too?"

Niamh smiled bravely at her. (She's so young, Tamsin thought, poor creature.) "I'm doing that now. It's all over, thank God. I hated her. But I didn't hurt her. I know I never could do that." Niamh let out a long breath.

Tamsin put a hand on her shoulder. "You'll do just fine. Now all you need is to stop making your pupils fall in love with you," she grinned.

Niamh dimpled with shyness. "I talked to the Head today. Apologised. He asked when I'd be ready to come back." She straightened up, chin held high. "I'll be back on Monday."

Tamsin had learnt what she needed to know. "I'm sorry you had such a hard time with that woman. She does seem to have had her own problems. But I'm glad to have heard your story. Glad you're exonerated."

"I'm kinda torn between hoping they catch whoever did this - cos it's wrong! - and .."

"Hoping they get away with it?"

"That sounds awful!"

"You needn't worry about it. I'm sure the police are closing in, and it's up to the law to decide then. All we need to do is ensure we let them know everything possible to ensure justice is done." Tamsin got up and headed to the door. "And you have. Good on you!" She let herself out.

But not without some misgivings. She hadn't told the police quite everything. But she didn't really have that much to tell - yet. Once they'd talked to Duncan Hattersley, she felt they'd be a good bit further forward.

CHAPTER THIRTY-ONE

It was late in the morning, after she'd finished a home visit to a couple with a barking dog. "He barks for no reason!" they had assured her. And she'd spent some time getting them to understand that dogs weren't mad, and just because we couldn't perceive the reason didn't mean a reason didn't exist! Once they grudgingly accepted that possibility, things went much more smoothly, and she left them with plenty of homework to do with their dog, and instructions to increase his sleeping hours by almost double. The poor little chap never rested and was living on his nerves.

She'd got back to Pippin Lane and opened her laptop to have a go at her accounts. She stared almost unseeing at the columns of numbers before her, sighing loudly enough to trouble Moonbeam. So when the phone rang and she could hear it was Feargal (his ringtone was the sound of typewriters clacking away), she slammed the laptop shut and eagerly snatched up her phone.

"Thought you'd want to know asap," he began. "Went to interview Duncan Hattersley this morning. I got him to show me round his property. He proudly showed off the statues in the niches. His grandfather carved them apparently - keen amateur artist."

"Oh, that's really interesting!"

"This is *more* interesting - when we walked to the far end of the house and saw the empty alcove, he nearly lost it entirely! 'Oh no, where's the saint gone?' and all that kind of thing. Said he'd had no idea it was missing."

"Did you believe him?"

"Frankly, no. My researches revealed that before he came to Great Malvern to take over his grandfather's house, he belonged to the Dudley Amateur Dramatic Society. Was a leading light in some of their productions."

"So he knows how to act!"

"He does. And he did it quite well. Except I noticed him eyeing me to see how I was taking his performance. Fatal mistake."

"That's cool! You did brilliantly!" enthused Tamsin. "Tell you what .. I'm going to go round and talk to him myself. I'll dream up something about the photography class or something."

"Don't go alone." There was a chill in Feargal's voice that made Tamsin shudder.

"Well I can't go with *you*."

"Where's Emerald today?"

"She's at some meditation day at the Buddhist Temple. I know! I'll take Charity. She can chatter about Malvern architecture, I'm quite sure. She can have a sudden interest in the decorated houses of that area."

"Let me know before you go in," said Feargal firmly. "I don't trust this Hattersley."

"Remember my Dachshund lady, Yvonne, has cameras watching the house!"

Tamsin rang off and got hold of Charity. "Want to try your hand at some sleuthing, Charity?"

"Ooh, lovely, dear - yes please!"

"I have to warn you, the person we're going to visit may possibly be the guilty party."

"We can manage him, I'm sure. You won't believe what my niece insisted I carry about with me? It's a personal alarm - it makes an almighty racket, quite deafening."

"Ok, be sure to have that with you. I really don't think he's going to go mad and lock us up. But I'm sure he has something to do with this business." Quickly bringing Charity up to speed over the whole statue saga, she arranged to pick her up a little later.

"I'll be in town anyway, dear. I hate to miss the Farmers' Market!"

This time, with Charity firmly on board, plus all her bags of fruit and veg, sourdough bread, and goats cheese from the Market, Tamsin pulled into the drive of the big house, parking beside an old brown Daimler. Before getting out of the van she buzzed a text to Feargal:

Bearding the lion in his den now.

Arriving at the front door, she turned to look up at Yvonne's house, and rising above it, the heavily-wooded slopes of the Worcestershire Beacon. The sun shone pleasantly. Straightening her shoulders and exchanging glances with Charity, she pulled the brass bell-pull. They heard movement in the house. The door opened and the ferrety-faced Duncan peered out at them myopically. He had thin grey hair combed over a tall thin pate. His grey flannel suit and dull shirt gave him a second-hand air. He pulled his glasses out of his breast pocket, and put them on. This all gave him time to think how to react to his visitors, Tamsin guessed.

"Ah, you're the dog-lady from Oliver's course, aren't you?"

"I am! Tamsin Kernick." He *can* act, she thought. He knows full well who I am. "And this is my friend Charity Cleveland. I was telling her about the program and how you're into Victorian architecture and lived in this road, and she got really excited to meet you."

"I did! Very excited!" nodded Charity.

"I'm flattered."

"I'm particularly interested in the houses along this road. It seems the architects were vying with each other to make their houses stand out."

"You're so right, Miss Cleveland. Do both come in," and with a flourish, Duncan invited them into his gloomy hallway. It was adorned with many pictures, mostly etchings of architecture, some from Malvern.

"Oh, how very interesting!" purred Charity, peering in the dark hall at one of the prints. "I do remember going to a children's party in that house - oh, many moons ago!" She smiled self-deprecatingly. "I expect you were still in short trousers then!" she tinkled a little laugh, and Duncan looked quite taken with her.

"Miss Cleveland, you flatter me again!" he simpered. Tamsin wondered if she'd need to rush outside to throw up if they went on like this.

She left Charity to get on with all the architectural small talk. She knew a surprising amount - about Malvern Stone, and the sort of bricks favoured by the Victorians, the ornately decorated barge-boards on the gable ends, and so on.

Only when a question of Charity's elicited the information that there were statues adorning this building did Tamsin jump in.

"Statues? I'd love to see them - may we?" she said animatedly.

"Certainly, my dear ladies, certainly," chuntered Duncan. "This way .." And he set off towards the front door.

"My grandfather was an artist and he carved them," he said with pride, as they arrived at the corner of the house where the first alcove was.

Charity ooh-ed and aah-ed very convincingly. Tamsin asked a question about who the subject was, Duncan gave a long explanation of who these statues were of - some mediaeval saints, it seemed. "See the flaming torch he's holding? He was burnt to death," said Duncan with undisguised glee. They shuffled on to the next alcove, the other side of the front porch.

Here there was more admiration, and more long stories. Tamsin, who was tiring of the history lesson, pointed to the far corner of the house. "Is there another one down here?"

"Er, yes. Yes, there's one more, it's another saint." And as they rounded the corner and gaped at the empty alcove, Duncan said, "Oh no! It's missing! How can that be?"

Tamsin was unimpressed by this unconvincing display, especially as she knew well that he had done the same routine for Feargal this morning. "That's dreadful! When did you last see it?"

"Oh, Ah, I can't be sure," he said, wringing his hands.

Charity piped up, "You don't think it's to do with those thefts, do you? You know, the random things being pinched?" She looked up at him, her eyes wide.

Duncan looked cornered.

Tamsin weighed in again. "You see, we found a bag of the stolen things, didn't we, Charity!"

"You did? Where?" he suddenly became interested again.

"Up on Midsummer Hill."

"On Midsummer Hill? Where was the bag? What sort of bag? Was it hidden?" He seemed unable to conceal his inappropriate interest.

"It was in the undergrowth somewhere ... can't remember where, can you, Charity?"

Charity got the message from Tamsin's eyes. "No, dear, I'm afraid I can't. It all looks the same, all that bracken, doesn't it!" she giggled.

"I wonder if the thief hid more stuff up there?" Tamsin wondered aloud.

"Not worth hunting for more clothes pegs and flower pots, though, is it," replied Charity.

Duncan was suddenly galvanised into action. "Now, you'll have to excuse me. I'm expecting a call soon that I need to take. It's been wonderful meeting you both," He put a hand in the small of each of their backs and propelled them firmly back towards the *Top Dogs* van. Tamsin turned before she reached her door saying, "Isn't it awful about that woman - er, Estelle!"

"Yes indeed, very bad, very bad," mumbled Duncan.

"Midsummer Hill - imagine! - that's the place where Estelle died!" she said sensationally. "What a coincidence!"

"So it is," said the agitated Duncan. "See you at the next class, Tamsin. A pleasure to make your acquaintance, Miss Cleveland." He gave a little bow.

And they at last obliged by getting into the van and turning to leave the property. Once clear of the house, Tamsin said, "You know where I'm going right now, Charity?"

"I have a sneaking suspicion that I do. I have to get back. I'm on the flower roster for the Harvest Festival tomorrow. Will you be safe?"

"I'll drop you back to your car on the top road, then I'll collect the dogs and head to the Hill. I'll text Feargal before I go. I promised ..."

And they whizzed up the hill towards Charity's little blue car.

By the time she'd sorted Charity and all her bags, and got home and organised the dogs, their harnesses, leads, her boots, and all the rest, she headed towards the Hills. And what should she see in the car park at the foot of Midsummer Hill, but a brown Daimler.

"Bingo!" she said under her breath. "We're in business, guys!" and she got them all out of the van. "Isn't it great when a plan works out?" The dogs couldn't care about plans. They just knew they were in dog heaven, and they went straight into sniff mode and scurried about, noses to the ground. The little group surged up the Hill, past the edge of the quarry, and heard the clanking of chains and the creak of leather.

A hefty snort reminded Tamsin what this was - it was Joe Bucket and his team of black horses, rolling the bracken. She called the dogs in and waved as she passed him. "I wondered if I'd be seeing you up here, Joe - the bracken is pretty thick up the top there."

"Ahh, indeed it be," he replied, "Can't stop m'dear. Takes too long to stop and start this rig," he cackled, his grin showing his long teeth, like tombstones in an old country graveyard, as he moved on past her, his weatherworn face shielded from the bright sunshine under his weatherbeaten tweed flat hat.

Tamsin ushered her gang past the horses and came out on the fort at the top of Midsummer. She walked round the earth ramparts. And there at the edge of the ancient warren, frantically rooting around in the bracken with a big stick, was Duncan Hattersley.

CHAPTER THIRTY-TWO

Duncan looked hot and bothered in the Autumn sun as he whacked and poked feverishly at the undergrowth. Even from a distance, Tamsin could see his thin grey hair sticking to his sweaty head. She signalled to her dogs to stay close. She had a sudden idea! Pulling a supermarket bag from her pocket - how handy that she was always ready to pick blackberries at this time of year! - she snatched up a handful of bracken and a couple of sticks and pushed them in to make the bag look long and thin.

Tamsin held the bag up in the air with both hands, making out that it was very heavy, and called out, "Is this what you're looking for?"

Duncan leapt like a startled rabbit, took in the sight of Tamsin and the bag, and after a second's delay he turned and bolted in the direction of the car park.

"Dogs!" she said urgently. The three dogs jumped up from where they'd been lying hidden in the bracken, ready for action. And feinting a throw, she shouted, "Go!"

All three dogs shot away in a straight line, which happened to be towards the running Duncan. Banjo was in the lead, hotly followed by Quiz, with Moonbeam putting on a surprising turn of speed to keep up with the bigger dogs as they pushed and bounced through the undergrowth.

The running man looked over his shoulder and, his face full of fear at the sight of the chasing dogs, he stumbled backwards. Putting his hand down to push off again, he regained his footing and turned to run away, just as Joe was bringing his team, chains clanking and leather creaking, over the brow of the hill. Seeing his new friend racing after her dogs and afraid she was in trouble, Joe whipped up his horses down the slope as Duncan ran straight towards him, still looking back over his shoulder at the advancing dogs. He was knocked flying.

"Whoa!" called Joe, "Who-o-o-a there!" He reined his team in as quickly as he could. The horses stopped with much snorting, stamping, and head-tossing, the runaway lying on his back just in front of their big feathered hooves. Tamsin, running after her panting dogs, had caught up.

Duncan looked up at seven pairs of eyes staring down at him, and with a big sigh fell back, defeated.

"Are you hurt?" asked Tamsin urgently as she stood over him.

Duncan closed his eyes.

"Nah, he's alright," Joe assured her. "He bounced off the leather collar. Your dogs gave 'im a rare ole fright! What's he running away from you for? I knew that were wrong, you being a good lady. Did he hurt you?"

"No, Joe. He didn't hurt me. But I'm pretty sure he hurt someone else. And the reason he was running was because he realised I'd sussed him out. Sit up!" she ordered Duncan.

He struggled up to a seated position.

"Got anything to tie him up with?" Tamsin asked Joe.

"I'm a gaaaarrrrdener, aren't I!" he winked, and drew a coil of blue baler twine from his pocket. "I thinks a hayman's knot will do nicely here," he added, as he tied Duncan's wrists behind his back, then attached the plastic twine to his heavy roller.

Tamsin was on the phone to Feargal. "... Yes, got him! He thought I'd found the statue Estelle had stolen, realised that I knew, and he ran away. ... Yep. Knew the game was up ... No, it's ok, I'm not alone. Joe Bucket is here with me. ... Joe! The one with the horses on the Hills! ... Ok, get the police and fetch yourselves up here." She gave him the precise location from her phone, and fished her cloth frisbee from its permanent parking place in her back pocket. She stepped away a little and started tossing the frisbee for her happy dogs, who were enjoying this more than usually stimulating walk.

Joe found a pair of nose-bags for his splendid black horses and they stood contentedly munching, Joe keeping an eye on their prisoner.

Duncan complained on and off. How it wasn't his fault; the rope was hurting his wrists (Joe checked it and was satisfied he was just being a fusspot); the ground was hard; Estelle was a nutcase and a trouble-maker and deserved what she got; she led him on about returning the statue then changed her mind, and so on. And on. And on.

Tamsin and Joe were beginning to tire of this extended lament when they heard the distant wail of a police siren.

"You'll be able to do all your moaning in the police station soon enough," said Tamsin, flicking a quick frisbee high in the air. Banjo ran and crouched beneath it, catching it handily and trotting back to her, not without a friendly warning growl at Moonbeam who was close beside him.

"So you never had the statue at all?" Duncan squinted up at Tamsin silhouetted against the bright open sky.

"The police have it. We know just what's been going on," she said, and turned her back on him to talk to Quiz.

Duncan, feeling ever more sorry for himself, went silent. And it wasn't long before they saw Feargal and two policemen in high-vis waistcoats clambering over the ramparts. As they arrived, the sergeant cautioned their prisoner, and with the help of Joe's pocket knife switched out his baler twine bracelets for standard-issue police handcuffs.

At this point Duncan found his voice again: "It was an accident! Honestly. She told me she'd give me back the statue if I didn't tell on her. Ow! These cuffs are too tight! Then she got snarky in the car park.

She went for me! I kinda lost it - you see it was my grandfather's statue ..." he pleaded. "It was an accident, I tell you!" and so he continued his pathetic wailing as he was walked away towards the police car between the two officers, their radios chattering scratchily and their bright yellow jackets gleaming in the sunlight.

"Don't push me about!" he shouted as they made their way across the grass. The quiet voice of the sergeant could faintly be heard, "We're just holding the cuffs so you don't trip, sir."

At last they disappeared down the Hill.

"Well done, kiddo!" said Feargal to Tamsin, then he stepped forward to shake Joe Bucket by the hand. "Thanks to you, we got our man!"

" 'Twas a fair cop!" said the old man. "Can't be running about like that without looking where you'm going." He shook his head sorrow-fully. "So what's he done? From all that racket he was making I'd say he's guilty as sin .. of whatever it is he's done."

"He killed a woman," said Tamsin, any sympathy she may have been feeling for the man ebbing away. "You know the woman who was found dead in the car park here? She'd been annoying a lot of people - a right pain. But you can't go round killing people because they're pests."

"There'd be a trail of dead bodies behind me if that were so," cackled Joe. "But at least I got a spade and knows how to bury 'em," he bent double as he wheezed with laughter.

"And there'd be a few people with sore heads pointing fingers at me too." Feargal joined in the merriment.

Tamsin turned to Feargal. "You see, he made out he didn't know the statue was missing."

"Again?"

"Again. Then his face lit up when I told him we'd found some of the stolen stuff on Midsummer Hill. Charity put the idea into his head that it had been in the bracken. I could see his mind whirring. So I dropped off Charity, fetched the dogs, and hot-footed it up here. Found him hunting for it."

"And why would he do that if he hadn't known who took it?"

"Exactly! That's what gave him away." Tamsin stroked the head of Banjo, who had cautiously sniffed Feargal's trouser-leg then returned to her side for safety. He may be Banjo's friend, but he was in a different place, and the dog wasn't taking any chances. "She'd told him she'd give it back to him. That's how they came to be here that day. Then she backtracked."

"Maybe he thought she was lying all along, and that's why he lost his rag and hit her."

"And then when I was at his house he realised she must have been telling the truth after all!"

They turned to walk away. "Joe - you've been amazing! Thank you. We must let you get on."

"Oh, ahh, that be alright. Happy to help." And as Tamsin gathered her dogs he called out, "Did you'm say Charity? That wouldn't be Charity Cleveland from Nether Trotley, would it?"

"It would indeed!" replied Tamsin with a broad smile, never surprised that everyone knew her friend.

"Now there was a lovely girl," he said quietly, nodding, "Ahh." Then he took the nosebags off his charges, picked up the reins and cried, "Walk on!" With a big heave the horses pulled hard into their collars, and the heavy roller creaked and started rolling again.

CHAPTER THIRTY-THREE

The Cake Stop was crammed. It was after the usual closing time, but on this occasion it was open for the launch of the photographic exhibition. Jean-Philippe and Kylie had spent ages hanging all the pictures, with Oliver Barnstaple standing back, tilting his head this way and that, saying "Up a bit," "Down a bit more," or "I think that one would be better over there."

At last it was as Oliver wanted - much to Jean-Philippe's relief, as his patience and equanimity were being sorely tested - and Tamsin and Emerald came to help add all the labels beneath each group of pictures. Everything was ready when the doors were opened at seven o'clock.

The notice had said "Entry free with a complimentary coffee". Damaris and both her sisters - Penelope and Electra - were there handing round dainty little cakes and delicate biscuits. Kylie was occupied with the coffee machine behind the counter, while Jean-Philippe became the expansive host, ushering people in and seeing that everyone had a drink.

There was a busy excited chatter, sounding quite different from the café's usual background hum of conversation. Most of the class students had brought a guest or two, and red dots were appearing on some of the photos. Niamh O'Connor was tasked with taking the orders and sticking on the dots. She looked content now, and found herself with a keen young helper in the form of Cameron. He quickly took over the dot-sticking, so the rows became rather wobbly. After he and his brothers had had a giggle at their portraits, they were intent on scoffing all the little cakes - but they were no match for Chas, who had eyes in the back of his head and issued stern warnings about pigs and early bedtime.

The two girls, Jessica and Chloe, never stirred from their position beside their display of model-esque images. On Oliver's insistence, their imaginative reflections photo was included.

Tamsin was just drifting from their display to Lucinda's. The images were predominantly green - close-ups of plants. Next to one rather ordinary-looking leaf was a photo of the drawing Lucinda had made from it.

"This is amazing!" she said to Emerald, who had appeared at her side. "Look at the drawing - it shows so much more than the photo. I wouldn't have believed it."

"Yes, you can see all the veins, subtle changes of colour - I like that little curvy bit where the leaf joins the stalk. You don't really notice it in the photo."

"Very clever ..." Then Tamsin saw Lucinda leaning forward to peer at a photo on another display. As soon as she became aware of Tamsin looking at her, she whipped off her glasses and stuffed them in her bag, smiling with embarrassment as she turned away. A penny dropped in Tamsin's mind, and she was glad.

The Furies' cakes looked superb in Damaris's photos. "These really look good enough to eat!" said a more relaxed Janice, who seemed rejuvenated without her grumpy sister to worry over.

"Oh thank you!" twittered Damaris, hopping from one foot to the other. "I have to say, dear, that you're looking so much better a couple months on from your awful loss. Time is a great healer," she added, and then blushed, as she wondered if she'd overstepped some social boundary. But taking a deep breath she pressed on, returning the compliment,

"And I love your landscape images!" She noticed that, unsurprisingly, of all the photos of the Malvern Hills Janice had submitted, not one was of Midsummer Hill. She admired a beautiful sunset view across to the Black Mountains before being boomed at by Penelope to come and refill her dish of cakes.

"Do you do birthday cakes?" asked a visitor, "only I have a special birthday coming up .." Damaris took her by the elbow and steered her towards Penelope, who'd be able to turn this enquiry into an order.

Tamsin heard the gruff voice of Joe Bucket behind her, "I don't 'old with this posh coffee. Give me a cup o' tea and a samwidge any day." She smiled and turned to find Charity berating him. "Joe Bucket. Will you ever change? You can have tea - I always do." She looked kindly at his wizened suntanned face and started leading him over to the counter, "I was sorry to hear about your mother ... long time ago, now ..."

Really, thought Tamsin, he's the salt of the earth, and she smiled.

A voice similar in boom-value to Penelope's sounded from near the window. "My best horse," said Grace Metcalfe, proudly indicating one of her photos. Her guests peered and nodded, and replied in similarly loud fashion.

Feargal sidled up to Tamsin. "Do you think they develop this mode of speech from yelling at each other over the sound of thundering hooves on the hunting-field?" he muttered from the side of his mouth.

She smiled back at him conspiratorially. "Hush! And look - how cute is that?" Molly and Saffron had lined up Amanda and Charlie's pushchairs beside each other. The babies chattered in babyspeak and offered each other their toys and bears. This friendship seemed to have got off to a flying start as Amanda gurgled and chuckled at her new playmate. She showed him her special giraffe, but snatched it away from his reach and clasped it close. "He'd better watch out," Molly said to Saffron, "she uses that giraffe like a shillelagh!"

Molly noticed Tamsin watching and said, "Talking of shillelaghs, isn't it great that Niamh has settled back in again."

"Splendid! Cameron still enamoured?" she asked quietly.

"All sorted. He still likes her, but differently. Oh, *Amanda!*" the mothers were distracted again by their charges. Tamsin looked over to the photos of bikes, and saw Mark proudly pointing them out to his mother Shirley.

"Heartwarming, isn't it?" she said to Feargal. "The mother who's done so much for her son."

"And he's repaying her well!" said Emerald, who'd come to join them, "Seems to have completely turned over a new leaf." She smiled coyly at their tall newspaperman friend. "I was just talking to those two girls," she added. "They're actually pretty bright. Not the airheads they make out to be. It's all part of the social influencer vibe apparently," she shook her head slowly.

"You're an old soul," Feargal teased. "But you're right - they'll do ok, that pair. They have, as they say, their finger on the pulse."

"But *I* want to stick on a red dot!" complained Joe loudly.

"I want to order copies of those portraits from Tamsin anyway," said Molly to Chas. "Can you sort that out with Niamh? Then each of them can stick on a red dot." And while he went to manage Red Dot Wars, Molly returned to Giraffe Wars from the pushchairs.

Alex bounced up to Tamsin, waving his arms, "Tamsin! Tamsin!" he yelled as if in the playground, "You've got more dots than anyone else!"

"Really?" she asked, and narrowing her eyes she looked across to her section, where the photo of Joe Bucket's horses against the bright blue of the sky had several dots below it. "Thanks for telling me, Alex," she beamed, and she grabbed hold of his shoulders as he was about to spin round, arms flailing, ensuring he narrowly missed the coffee cups on a nearby table.

After an hour the crowd had thinned out. Tamsin saw that just Emerald and Feargal, along with Charity, Lucinda, and Oliver were left. Niamh handed her list of purchasers over to their teacher to manage, and Chas started to herd his family towards the door. Niamh hurried out after them.

Jean-Philippe was passing close by. "Jean-Philippe! This is a splendid show you've put on," Tamsin called out to him.

"*Mais oui!*" he responded. "And it's brought me a few bookings! A birthday party in the upper room, and *Olivair* wishes to run another program in the spring. All down to your inspiration," he made a deep bow.

Tamsin looked suitably abashed. "Is it possible to purchase coffees now? I know it's late, but I'm whacked, and I'd love to collapse in those inviting armchairs ..."

"*Biensûr.* It will take a while to restore all the tables and chairs to their rightful places. As long as you don't mind us sweeping round you?"

"I can help shove chairs about," Feargal volunteered.

"*Merci*, Feargal! Then Kylie can fix your drinks. But," he enquired mockingly of Tamsin, "you cannot drink coffee without your faithful friends beside you?"

"I cannot! They're in the van. I'll run and get them now!"

And so they all wound up sitting in the window seats, the street outside now dark but lamplit. Oliver had crept over, rubbing his hands together, and said, "May I join you?" rather sheepishly. Once they were all settled with a welcome mug of coffee and had celebrated the success of the exhibition, inevitably the conversation turned to the non-exhibitor, the unfortunate Duncan Hattersley.

"Five years in prison and a life for the sake of a bit of carving," sighed Lucinda.

Tamsin was quick to reply, "People have their priorities all wrong. If only they paid more attention to their dogs and less to their worldly goods, we'd all be better off."

"Will he really get five years?" asked Charity.

"Manslaughter's usually somewhere between two and ten years," Feargal explained. "We'll have to wait for sentencing to see what he gets."

"They accepted it as manslaughter then, not murder?"

"Yes, they did. Don't think the weasel is bright enough to plot a decent murder," he grinned.

"I still don't get what exactly happened," said Lucinda, leaning forward.

And they all turned expectantly to Tamsin.

CHAPTER THIRTY-FOUR

Tamsin leant back in her armchair, hopped Moonbeam onto her lap and sighed. "Ok. Here's what you may not know. It seems that Duncan was very fond of his grandfather's carvings, which were housed in alcoves around his house. He discovered one missing, coincidentally the morning of Oliver's first class." She glanced towards the photography teacher, who was anxiously kneading his chubby fingers. "He'd been following the reports in the *Malvern Mercury* about all the snaffling that was going on, and started to do his own snooping. He noticed this figure trailing her shopping trolley around frequently, and started to log her whereabouts, then compare them with the reports in the *Mercury*."

Feargal jumped in, "Who says local papers don't have a part to play in local life?"

"Too right. Well he found out via Grace Metcalfe whom he knew, that Estelle was in the photography class, and enrolled for the following week. This gave him even more possibilities to track her, with the assignment we were given." Tamsin stroked Moonbeam's head thoughtfully. "He reckoned he knew it was she who'd pinched his statue, and he challenged her. He says she admitted it and would take him to where it was. He drove her to Midsummer Hill. He says that when they arrived she changed her mind and laughed at him. He lost his temper, she made to attack him, and he shoved her ... When he saw what he'd done he bolted."

"Sounds like him alright," said Charity.

"Meanwhile, Charity and I had found a bag of Estelle's thievings up on the Hill, and handed them in to the police. With the aid of a friend's CCTV footage, we could actually see Estelle going into Duncan's drive, then emerging a while later with a much heavier trolley bumping along behind her."

"Wow! Bet the police were glad of those tapes!" said Lucinda.

"They were. So when Charity and I went round to talk to Duncan, we hinted that the statue may have been hidden on the Hill, as we'd already found other stuff in a carrier bag hidden there. We told no lies, but in fact, I'd already done a search of the hilltop with my dogs, and found the missing statue."

There was a gasp from the assembled company.

"That's extraordinary!"

"Brilliant dogs!"

"I had no idea you were that clever!"

Tamsin shifted uncomfortably in her seat, and re-adjusted Moonbeam on her lap. "And that went to the police too."

She continued, "So he took the bait and went straight up the Hill to look for his statue. What he hadn't realised was that his suspicion tied him to the murder. It wasn't till he saw me up there that the penny dropped, that he'd fallen into the trap. That's why he ran."

"This really is like being in a crime drama!" Oliver said, patting his chubby knees with the flat of his hands.

"So then it was just a case of sending the dogs after him," Tamsin smiled fondly at her sleeping dogs.

"And Joe Bucket appearing with his horses at just the right moment!" chuckled Emerald.

"Once he realised he was caught he resigned himself to his fate."

"But not," said Feargal emphatically, "without a lot of whingeing and protesting that it wasn't his fault."

They were all quiet for a moment.

"I can't see how he can avoid a custodial sentence," Oliver put in.

"Well, he's likely to get a few years," said Feargal. "You can't go around killing people - however bats they may be."

"Toldya there was something in this petty thieving!" Tamsin grinned at him.

Lucinda chewed her lip. "But why did she do it?"

"Some form of kleptomania, apparently. They pinch things they have no need of. Commonly raises its head in later years."

"That would explain her tetchiness," said Emerald, "pinching all this stuff without wanting any of it. Feeling out of control."

"Do you think it was some sort of cry for help?" asked Lucinda.

"Could have been," Tamsin shrugged. "It was a compulsion. I imagine she enjoyed the buzz - feeling important for once in her life, not overshadowed by her older sister."

"And it gradually built up to taking things of value," Lucinda nodded.

"Did you suspect him right away?"

"We suspected everyone. Actually you were on our list, Lucinda! There were photos - from the assignment - of you secreting something in your bag." Lucinda looked nonplussed, so Emerald found the photo in Tamsin's phone to show her.

"Oh! That's me hiding my glasses. I'm afraid I'm awfully vain about them. I hate them, actually, and wear them as little as possible."

"I noticed that," Tamsin smiled, "earlier on this evening."

"I know it's silly, but it's something about being an artist. I feel I don't want people to see my weakness. But you all know now." She blushed and looked down at her lap. "Look," she said, putting her hand into her bag and fishing out her tapestry glasses case, "Here they are. Is that what you can see in the picture?"

"Oh yeah, that's what you're holding," grinned Emerald.

"There were others too, not just you! But I don't want to disclose their secrets." Tamsin was thinking of Niamh O'Connor and her young admirer, Cameron. "If they choose to tell you, that's up to them."

"We even wondered what was going on with Saffron," said Feargal. "Remember that photo you had of her frantically refilling her dropped bag in the market, looking so guilty?"

"Oh, I was just chatting to her about that earlier, over the pushchair camp," said Emerald. "She was embarrassed because the .. er .. feminine products she'd just bought had spilled all over the pavement when she dropped her bags!"

"Dear Saffron!" exclaimed Charity. "I didn't know she was so shy about such things."

"She produced some nice photos in the end. That's a gorgeous one of an interior with the baby on the carpet," Lucinda spoke warmly.

"Once we'd worked on the composition to remove the dirty crocks and old nappies," Oliver grinned and glanced around him, beginning to feel quite at home in this group.

"Everyone's worldview is so different," said Charity. "Look at all these pictures. They're all so different, different subjects, different approach ..."

"That's where the art comes in," said Oliver proudly. "It's not just a question of cataloguing what you see. Looking at things differently is our aim."

"And looking at things differently is what Tamsin does best," murmured Feargal.

"All I know is that we would never have cracked this without Quiz, Banjo, and Moonbeam." Quiz raised her head at her name, saw nothing much happening, sighed and lay down again. "Know what, Feargal? I'm going to write my next article for the *Malvern Mercury* on scent games people can play with their dogs!"

"Great idea!" Feargal nodded approvingly.

"You'll have some terrific pictures to illustrate it now ... *and* your book," added Emerald. Tamsin smiled back at her, grateful for the encouragement for her book project.

"Ooh, Muffin will love that," cooed Charity, wriggling in her chair.

"Malvern will be crawling with sniffer dogs!" laughed Lucinda.

"*Alors!* No peace for the wicked!" said Jean-Philippe, his hands leaning on the back of Feargal's chair.

"To Quiz, Banjo, and Moonbeam!" said Oliver, raising his empty mug.

"Quiz, Banjo, and Moonbeam!" everyone echoed happily, and they all drank a coffee toast to the dozing dogs.

Ready for Christmas Carols and Canine Capers - *the next book in this popular series? You'll find it here:*

https://mybook.to/Christmascozy

^^^ Scan the code above or click here

" A Howling Good Christmas Mystery!

In the heart of England's Malvern Hills, Tamsin Kernick faces more holiday havoc when a festive gathering of inept but well-meaning carol singers ends in murder. While it's a silent night for the victim, the merry gentlemen (and gentlewomen) of the choir find themselves under intense scrutiny.

Eager to collar the criminal so her friends can enjoy their mince pies and Christmas holiday, dog trainer Tamsin and her super-sleuthing dogs race against the clock to get the culprit locked up before the Man in Red arrives. As the jingle bells of approaching police cars draw near, Tamsin is determined to restore sweet singing in the choir.

Can Tamsin and her canine companions unwrap the mystery and bring joy back to their cozy town?

Christmas Carols and Canine Capers! is the delightful seventh book in the Tamsin Kernick English Cozy Mystery series. If you love quirky characters, gentle clean mysteries, and a dash of Christmas cheer, you'll adore this festive caper.

To find out how Tamsin arrived in Malvern and began Top Dogs, you can read this free novella "Where it all began" at
https://urlgeni.us/Lucyemblemcozy
and we'll be able to let you know when Tamsin's next adventure is ready for you!

And if you enjoyed this book, I'd love it if you could whiz over to where you bought it and leave a brief review, so others may find it and enjoy it as well, and be kind to their animals!

ALL THE TAMSIN KERNICK COZY ENGLISH MYSTERIES

Where it all began ..
https://urlgeni.us/Lucyemblemcozy

Sit, Stay, Murder!
https://mybook.to/SitStayMurder

Ready, Aim, Woof!
https://mybook.to/ReadyAimWoof

Down Dog!
https://mybook.to/downdog

Barks, Bikes, and Bodies!
https://mybook.to/BarksBikesBodies

Ma-ah, Ma-ah, Murder!
https://mybook.to/TamsinKernickCozies

Snapped and Framed!
https://mybook.to/SnappedFramed

Christmas Carols and Canine Capers! A Howling Good Christmas Mystery!
https://mybook.to/Christmascozy

Also available in Large Print
https://mybook.to/TamsinKernickCozies

ABOUT THE AUTHOR

From an early age I loved animals. From doing "showjumping" in the back garden with Simon, the long-suffering family pet - many years before Dog Agility was invented - I worked in the creative arts till I came back to my first love and qualified as a dog trainer.

Working for years with thousands of dogs and their colourful owners - from every walk of life - I found that their fancies and foibles, their doings and their undoings, served to inspire this series of cozy mysteries.

While the varying characters weave their way through the books, some becoming established personnel in the stories, the stars of the show are the animals!

They don't have human powers. They don't need to. They have plenty of powers of their own, which need only patience and kindness to bring out and enjoy with them.

If you enjoyed this story, I would LOVE it if you could hop over to where you purchased your book and leave a brief review!

Lucy Emblem

Printed in Great Britain
by Amazon